About the Author

Michael John Wilde's journey is almost as colourful as his latest character, Billy Chen, having experienced a host of adventures travelling throughout the world. Michael has created a number of characters who appeal to children of all ages. For readers from nine to ninety, his stories resonate and entertain.

Billy Chen and The Holy Wars

Michael John Wilde

Billy Chen and The Holy Wars

Olympia Publishers

London

www.olympiapublishers.com
OLYMPIA PAPERBACK EDITION

A CIP catalogue record for this title is
available from the British Library.

ISBN: 978-1-78830-100-8

This is a work of fiction.
Names, characters, places and incidents originate from the writer's
imagination. Any resemblance to actual persons, living or dead, is purely
coincidental.

First Published in **2018**

Olympia Publishers
60 Cannon Street
London
EC4N 6NP

Printed in Great Britain

Dedication

This is the first in a number of stories following the adventures of Billy Chen. Dedicated to my children, Jacqui, Rob, Anna, Molly, CoCo, Imo and Gus, who have given me a lasting reason to seek magic from today and hope for the future.

Preface

Both hands on the illuminated face of Big Ben edged towards the Roman numeral twelve, ready for the Great Bell to welcome another freezing January day. Not just welcoming another day, but, later, hastening the arrival of the first passenger flight from New York, of the massive new Pan Am Boeing 747. Pan Am's first transatlantic flight had been dogged with technical delays, and was already expected to arrive several hours late into Heathrow. Every minute the flight's arrival was delayed was proving a godsend to one lonely soul. For he was determined to stop Irish terrorists from blowing up the gleaming new Pan Am Jumbo on its arrival into Heathrow. On his arrival from 2016 AD, Billy Chen had begged the police to listen to his pleas to re-route the incoming inaugural flight from New York; and,if they would not, then to heed his warning that IRA hot shots were waiting in Hounslow on the roof of Dennison House, a high rise office building along the Bath Road. Their undetected position on the easterly flight path allowed an easy shot with a SAM missile at the incoming Pan Am flight.

From research Billy had carried out back in Liverpool in 2016 AD, he was certain of his facts. In fourteen hours, after the Great Bell had welcomed another day, Boeing's latest creation would pass within a few miles of the Elizabeth Tower, housing Big Ben, London's best known landmark. Unless Billy could convince the 1970s police, the IRA would score their biggest victory on British soil, blowing Pan Am's new 747 into a million pieces over highly populated housing, just to the east of Heathrow.

Billy's Triumph Bonneville skidded to a halt in Cranford, along Byron Avenue, close by Dennison House, secretly occupied by the waiting IRA terrorists. Technical problems, causing Pan Am's inaugural flight to be delayed until early afternoon, had allowed Billy a chance to consider how to save all of those on board. Billy had watched matters unfold at Heathrow, on his electronic time portal wizardry, back home in his mother's Liverpool terraced house. Realising the immediate danger, he sped back through time to January 1970, knowing that he was the only one aware of the military plan hatched by a group of determined IRA terrorists.

Billy had a passion for air travel. His unique time-travelling capabilities had led him to attend several moments of aviation history. He'd watched at Boscombe Down, in Wiltshire, as the first RAF Harrier Jump Jet had been put through its paces. Posing as a member of the ground crew technical team, he stood close by, as the revolutionary war plane was shown off, eerily hovering a short distance from a host of Royal Air Force dignitaries. Further back in history, on the 17th December 1903, at Kitty

Hawk, North Carolina, Billy had watched as the Wright Brothers had made the first controlled powered flight. On that misty morning man's adhesion to terra firma was broken forever.

But events in 1970 were totally different; now there was clear and present danger, albeit forty-six years in the past. He could not sit and watch as hundreds of innocent passengers and crew were slaughtered. The implications in history would reach well past his comprehension. There was nothing in the history books to prove that this tragedy had taken place. For some reason Billy had been placed in a situation; for the first time he must act for the good of mankind.

There was only one way to ensure the course of history was left undisturbed. Just a few hours from now, across the west of London, on the populated approach to Heathrow, death and destruction would certainly occur. Billy's wizardry in creating computer games, now in App form, must be the only way to save the situation. With his available time continuum technology, he could watch events in real time; plus, he had the opportunity to move through his own time portal, to events in 1970, or wherever he chose. Billy sat in his bedroom, with his faithful Apple iMac and several TV screens, each one tuned to different events in time. Two of his screens provided images of the roof top of Dennison House along the Bath Road, currently at eight a.m. on January 22nd, 1970. Another split screen showed the approaches to Heathrow on runway 27R and 27L, in real time eight a.m. in 2016.

To Billy, the answer was simple. Using his time portal, he would create an App game. This would lift the waiting terrorists into his App, allowing them to destroy an airborne target within the new game. But first, he must ensure that full details of the

App were spot on. The incoming flight must be checked, and the type of rocket launcher which the IRA fighters intended to use; both must be loaded into the App. Once this information had been entered into the game, his task would be to move the terrorists through the time portal, capturing them within his new game. Once there, they could blow up whatever target they chose; that's if they had the relevant skills and could overcome the dangers which Billy would set. For, as in all good computer games, life would not be easy for the attacker. They would face a SWAT team armed with the latest laser weaponry, who would, in turn, be seeking to destroy them. All Billy could do was push ahead with his new App. Real time was whizzing by; there were now just two hours before flight PA 001 from New York, with three hundred and twenty-four passengers on board, would make its final approach into range of a waiting SAM missile.

With the IRA terrorists locked into an image on Billy's real time screen, with a border surrounding them, Billy dragged them into his new App already prepared, waiting on his Apple iMac. The rest would be played out as Billy's latest App – *Flight Path*.

Twenty-five heavily armed SWOT security men swung across the screen within *Flight Path*, surrounding the IRA terrorists, all six having no chance to resist the surprise attack. Both SAM missiles were forced from the control of the terrorists, and then instantly disarmed – extra points. Now under the control of the SWOT team, all six of the terrorists were dragged from the roof. Each one disappeared into a section of the screen, the home for losers. Their loss achieved a victory for the SWOT team, clocking up winner's points on the left of the screen. Across the top of the screen, a Pan Am Boeing 747, wheels fully extended, lowered itself onto to runway 27L. Billy's new airport App, *Flight Path*, based on actual events on January 22nd 1970 – with a few of Billy's changes – was ready for release to the public.

CHAPTER ONE

Oh Yeah... it really does start like this... the fun stuff awaits you
The Middle Ages in the Kingdom of Palogonia
"Once upon a time..."

Many years ago, in the kingdom of Palogonia, a Princess called Xena lived all alone, imprisoned in the secluded wing of a medieval castle. She had been locked away by her depraved mother, Queen Ventenil, to ensure that she would never become Queen. Princess Xena's twins, Axle and Imogena, had been taken from her when they were just a few months old, to live in the royal quarters, along with their grandmother, QueenVentenil. Princess Xena's husband, Prince Gandolf, had never returned from the Great Crusades in The Holy Land, which he had undertaken in an attempt to free Jerusalem from the Muslim Seljuk Turkish Armies. News was returned to Xena, via her mother, that her husband had been killed in a lengthy battle to free the Christian shrine.

She had mourned for nearly ten years, dressed only in funereal black, locked away from the world and her children. Xena was a beautiful lady; her long black hair shone, even without the sunlight for which she hankered. Even the ravages from years of solitary mourning had removed little of her beauty and elegance. Her mother, Queen Ventenil, was an angry, cold-hearted woman, past the bloom of youth, yet still dressed in an attempt to reflect her beauty of years past. Both twins were kept from their mother, brought up by nannies and castle staff, all sworn to secrecy. Queen Ventenil cosseted her grandchildren well away from their grieving mother. As they grew, knowing little else, both children began to rely on the security and guidance of the Queen.

On their fifth birthday, the Queen summoned the children to her quarters. There she informed them their parents had died shortly after they were born. Determined to keep the secret, she would hide their mother away forever. For Queen Ventenil had forced Gayla, a dangerous black witch, to spike Xena's food and water. The magic potion would leave the rightful heir to the throne in a trance, mourning her dead husband forever. Its magic powers would keep her in limbo, unaware of her past life, her children, and unable to speak or think clearly. But, as with all magic spells, Gayla advised the Queen that every spell cast could be broken. For if Prince Gandolf's wedding band was placed in Xena's left palm, she would be returned to her children, taking her rightful place as Queen. On hearing the witch's predictions, Queen Ventenil laughed out loud, believing that her daughter would die in her imprisoned quarters. For she was certain that her son-in-law's ring would be lying in some distant land, amongst the fallen bodies of many of Palogonia's brave soldiers.

On reaching their tenth birthdays in 1192 AD, the twins' thoughts of their parents, although continually curious, were slipping away with the passing of time. For their grandmother refused to discuss her only child or their father, Prince Gandolf, whom the Queen had always considered unsuitable to marry her daughter. Prince Gandolf was the only surviving son of King Alfred, the wise and much loved ruler of the rich and peaceful Kingdom of Castonia, a friendly nation, situated over the Black Mountains that separated their two Kingdoms.

QueenVentenil had ruled Palogonia for nearly ten years since her husband King Bresdon had died tragically. The King had suspiciously fallen from the castle fortifications early one morning, whilst making his pre-breakfast inspection of the ramparts. King Bresdon was loved by all his subjects. He worked tirelessly to ensure that everyone shared in the prosperity of his Kingdom, all achieved under his five-year reign. But on his death, Queen Ventenil had claimed the throne from her daughter, declaring Xena insane, and therefore unsuitable to rule Palogonia. Initially, there was no issue, as the people were happy with their lives. Each shared in the prosperity which King Bresdon had created, offering a comfortable existence for everyone.

But just a few months after Queen Ventenil grabbed control of the throne, she ordered all her ministers and generals to swear allegiance to her, their new Queen. Her first action as ruler was to impose sweeping new taxes on all her subjects. Her new levies took at least seventy percent of all money, property, live stock and crops away from her beleaguered subjects. Overnight, a Kingdom where laughter could be heard resounding across the fields, and where children were permitted to play in the castle grounds, changed. A silence spread over the Kingdom – bitterness grew towards Queen Ventenil and anyone residing within the castle defences.

The castle had been the home of the reigning sovereign for over five hundred years, and stood proudly on a hill, peering across the verdant flatlands below. The farmland spread as far as the Black Mountains and on either side of the Palo River; there, tireless workers lovingly grew a variety of crops. Their toils provided sufficient food to feed the whole Kingdom, with a surplus ensuring that large stores of food could be kept in reserve, should a poor harvest occur. In fact, it was a Utopian Kingdom, all created by the wisdom of King Bresdon. During his reign, workers sang as they toiled away each day, happy in the knowledge that they were sharing a wealth which their efforts were creating. As they went about their business working the Kingdom's verdant farmland, most were oblivious to the lives of their masters, who lived behind the defences of the castle. Most noblemen were proud to take up arms and lead the King's army, forming part of a coalition of the Kingdom's close allies against the heathens who were destroying the Holy Lands. Each was determined to fight anyone endangering their peace and security. But although they were loyal citizens, many failed to understand why the King's forces were sent to fight in the Holy Lands. For months, they would journey just to reach these bloody battlefields, there to fight against an evil force which, their leaders advised, was taking away the rights and beliefs of good Christian men. As a devout Christian, King Bresdon believed in the Papal request to protect the Holy Lands of Jerusalem as his duty. Many strong young men from the fields, some eager to join the army, made up a formidable fighting force. All wished to join the coalition with neighbouring like-minded Christian Kingdoms.

But now, under the rule of the hated Queen Ventenil, even the children could sense the unrest amongst the village folk. Unperturbed by the evil Queen, village life went on, whilst angry villagers sought ways to hide their assets away from the prying eyes of QueenVentenil's tax collectors. Scruffy urchins still scampered between their mothers' legs, young girls giggled as they carried water, purposefully aware of their attraction to the young farm workers. Elders sat and talked with affection of the late King Bresdon and other masters long gone, of bloody battles fought in distant lands, and of comrades who had failed to make the journey home. Life drifted by. For many years, under King Bresdon, life came and went in a world unscathed by the tribulations of wealth, greed and power. But all had changed. Now the talk amongst the elders was of how they could escape the horrors that Queen Ventenil had thrust upon the villagers.

CHAPTER TWO

Get me out of here
1192 AD
The Kingdom of Palogonia

Princess Xena's children, Axle and Imogena, had, for ages, hankered to venture away from the castle and meet the folk who lived below, in the workers' cottages that permeated the landscape. They stood for hours at the ramparts, considering how to explore the Kingdom below, which spread as far as the eye could see, towards the Black Mountains. Both yearned to join the village children, learning how to participate in the strange games that appeared to occupy their play times. But would the children speak to them? Would they speak the same language? Would they be in any danger? For the young royals had no idea of the depth of feelings against their grandmother, who was now, by far, the most hated person in the Kingdom.

As for all children, the risk of adventure was too great a challenge to miss. Carefully, they planned their break-out, excited at the prospect of the adventures which their visit outside the walls would bring them. Their plan was relatively simple; for, each day, two horse-drawn wagons left the castle, laden with lordly household waste. They would secrete themselves on one of the wagons, and, when far enough from the castle, jump from their hiding place, running into the dense pine woods for cover. They went over and over their plan; it was foolproof. Nothing could go wrong. They would be free to run and play, roll happily in the fields like normal children, maybe climb trees – their lives would be filled with happiness. Free from the confines of the castle, Grandmother's ever-watchful eye, and the boredom of Gerald, their droning old tutor. History, Latin, Scripture, Literature: the lessons were endless. And then there was music. Oh dear, how they giggled as Matilda, their music tutor, sang insanely to herself about Sweet Nightingales. What lessons did the children in the valley have to suffer? Surely more interesting than theirs! Anything must be better.

As the sun appeared over the castle walls, the twins slid from their beds, already dressed, prepared for their escape. Grandmother always slept till late each morning, and their servants would be too busy making fires and readying the dining room for breakfast.

CHAPTER THREE

Be patient and all will become clear.
Still in the Middle Ages
The Kingdom of Palogonia

Martha Castleman had lived all her life in the family's tiny cottage, below the castle walls. She understood that her great-grandfather had originally built the house with materials supplied by King Bresdon's father, King Raul II. Workers' cottages usually stayed within the family for several generations, so little had changed. Her accommodation was simple: just one open space, separated by a threadbare sack curtain, with a fireplace which fed its smoke through a hole in the roof – it was home. Martha was now without her beloved father, who had died the previous Christmas from a plague that had swept through the village. Their home was warm and dry; there, Martha, her mother, and her brother, Jasper, lived and laughed together. But the Castleman family was little different from all others living outside the castle. Much talk was now of Queen Ventenil, and of how they could secrete their assets away from the prying eyes of her tax collectors. Once, they had been a proud part of a community spirit. Then, everyone had stored surplus food, and had shared with other families when times were tough. But the Queen's new laws had forced everyone to become more inward looking, sadly, thinking only of their immediate family.

Martha had friends who had never returned from the first Holy Crusade five years earlier, but, unlike Princess Xena's, her mourning was different. For Martha had a family to support and ensure they had food, shelter and a chance to survive. Martha's younger brother Jasper, now eighteen, was forced into joining the army. Jasper was not a strong boy, born with a malformed left ankle, leaving his foot pointing at a weird angle. His disability made it difficult for him to walk at any speed. It was obvious that Jasper was never going to make a front-line fighting soldier. When he was taken to the castle to be conscripted into the army, he was told that he would probably become a cook. Although Jasper was disfigured, the thought that he would be unable to fight, alongside others from the Kingdom, made him understandably angry. Martha's comforting words had little meaning, but deep down she knew that there was a reasonable chance her brother would return from the pointless wars. Feeding stations for the troops would be way back from the front line, where endless bloody battles would be raging. Martha had lost many friends, although there was no evidence that they had perished in the Holy Lands. But the thought of losing her crippled brother as a front line soldier was too much to contemplate.

Unlike most of the villagers, Martha could read and write. As a teenager, she had worked in the castle. Her task each day was to clean the rooms of the royal children's tutor, her close friend Gerald. Gerald was a kindly man who loved to spread his vast knowledge to anyone prepared to listen. Martha was a perfect target, only too willing to absorb the great secrets which Gerald's books could offer. For five years, Martha made time to ensure that she spent every possible minute in Gerald's company, studying his collection of learned books. When well into her teens, Martha could read the Bible, work out numbers, and read stories for those in the village, who would hang on her every word, most mesmerised by her talents.

Keen to share her knowledge, Martha taught any of the village children who wanted rudimentary reading and writing skills. Rapidly, Martha developed a following, teaching those children whose families wanted their offspring to gain her mystical knowledge. But many families were wary of this strange behaviour, most considering that reading and writing to be the devil's work. Some kept their distance from Martha, whose talents had branded her as a white witch. Unknown to those suspicious of her abilities, Gerald had coached Martha into many of his mystic skills. By her eighteenth birthday, in 1192 AD, Gerald had passed on many of his secrets, hinting at the adventures which she was soon to encounter.

CHAPTER FOUR

Prince Axle and Princess Imogena join our story...
1192 AD
The Kingdom of Palogonia

As the cart containing Axle and Imogena rumbled its way down from the castle, hauled by a giant black cart horse, the royal twins clung desperately to the undercarriage of the creaking garbage wagon. They had never encountered such a stench, as the overfilled barrels spilled over them, lying cramped and hidden from view. Overnight, the twins had been woken by flashes of lightning and endless claps of thunder, which had set all the dogs scampering around the castle, howling in fear at the deafening racket. The downpour that followed the storm had filled the shallow drainage ditches, and had flooded potholes now enlarged by the torrential rain. By the time the twins had reached what they perceived as safety, they were drenched to the skin and layered with a stinking covering of mud. A far look from the pristine and courtly clothing into which they were forced everyday. Now they could pass as any raggamuffins living and working outside the castle. Surely they must now be safe. The creaking and bouncing cart slowed, eventually coming to a halt at the edge of the pine forest.

"Morning, Jed," Seth's rasping voice sounded from above them.

"S'pose it is, come on then," Jed offered a disinterested curt reply.

"Better feed the 'orse first," Seth suggested, patting the sweating cart horse, already agitated as it waited for a nose bag to be attached with its morning feed of dried oats.

Now must be their time to escape. Axle gestured to his sister for silence, fearful that they would be captured and taken back to the castle in disgrace, to face the wrath of their unforgiving grandmother. But it was now or never. For they had clearly reached the spot where the two men were going to empty the stinking garbage wagon.

"Follow me… don't say a word," Axle ordered in a whisper, as he eased his sister down onto the muddy track.

Slowly, they crawled away from under the cart, just praying that the squelching of the mud thickened by last night's deluge would not be heard. They were in luck. Jed and Seth were now fully preoccupied with attaching a nosebag to the restless cart horse. With the two men fully occupied, the two royal children carefully made their way from under the wagon, towards the nearby safety of the pineforest.

"Phew, that was close," Axle exhaled. "What a mess. How do we get this mud off?"

"Axle, the mud's not important; don't you realise? We've escaped! We're out of that dreadful castle! This is wonderful," his sister replied, spinning round, mud dropping from her sodden clothing.

"An' where do yuh youngsters think yuh're running off to?" Jed's massive frame stood blocking their way from entering further into the woods.

"Don't let the little rascals go, the Queen'll 'ave my 'ead," Seth bellowed from behind Jed.

"I got 'em, they aint goin' nowhere." Jed turned to Seth, smug in the knowledge that the two princes were cornered, their escape to explore the countryside completely blocked.

Axle and Imogena cowered down, both shaking with the realisation that there was no escape from the two angry garbage men, who were towering over them. Big, big trouble was now on the horizon. Once the two oafs had returned them to the castle, for certain they would face the endless wrath of their grandmother. She would remove all their privileges, and would most certainly ground them for several weeks. They recalled the last time they had broken grandmother's strict house rules. Together with being grounded for several weeks, she'd imposed extra punishment and extra lesson time, with the emphasis on written Latin.

Jed stumbled back from the cart, dragging a net which would easily hold the two escaping twins. Jed was never going to let the twins escape into the pine forest. Eventually Queen Ventenil would work out, maybe with the aid of Gayla, that Jed's garbage cart was the transport which had been used to make their escape. Once he returned the royal twins back inside the castle grounds, Jed would threaten one of the new maids to scrub the filth from the two children, only then would he ensure that they were locked back securely in the castle.

There was no escaping either the blinding flash or the shock waves which followed, tumbling Jed and Seth headlong into the surrounding blackberry brambles. As they scrambled to their feet, tearing off the brambles, first onto their knees and, then, wobbling to their full height, all that remained, where the two princes had stood, was a silver glow shimmering on the muddy track.

CHAPTER FIVE

"When you walk through a storm, hold your head up high"
2016 AD
Liverpool

"Up you get, kids! They'll be still looking for you eight hundred years ago; you're safe here." Billy Chen offered his hand to Axle and Imogena, both still shaken from their experiences escaping from their grandmother. Axle and Imogena stared in disbelief at Billy's strange clothing: a red and white Liverpool Football Club scarf knotted round his neck, and a matching baseball cap covered with metal badges from bygone matches throughout Europe. His words were almost drowned out by piped music belting from the Liverpool FC supporters shop, delivering *"You'll never walk alone"* to the surrounding area. Added to Gerry Marsden's rendition of the club anthem, a pre-recorded roar of some forty thousand voices, offering strange sounds, like nothing the two mystified royal kids had ever experienced before.

Appearing from Liverpool's Club Shop, two confused royal kids stood huddled together, trying to make sense of what had occurred following the silvery flash. Their medieval mud-splattered clothing had disappeared. Both were now somehow bedecked in black tracksuit bottoms, branded Stevie Gerrard first team shirts, LFC badged anoraks, and red and black scarves emblazoned with, *"You'll never walk alone"*. Billy proudly admired his two new scouser lookalikes, as they wobbled around, struggling to come to terms with their new red and white Nike trainers. Two frightened royal children were now urgently needing an explanation of their unbelievable change of circumstances, having whizzed through Billy's time portal to 2016 AD.

"It's OK, guys; you're safe here. You're at Anfield, the home of football. Confused, hey?" Billy started to explain. "I was scared when I first made the journey," Billy offered, leading them into an empty club room.

Axle squeezed his sister's hand, as, nervously, they followed Billy. Cautiously, they stared into a room decorated with yet more colourful scarves and photographs of young men wearing shirts similar to theirs. Against one wall, a giant television screen looked down on the twins, showing yet more young men running around wearing red shirts and very short red trousers. It seemed that, with every breath, yet another new experience was unfolding before them.

"Alex, you and your sister sit here and watch." Billy pointed to a row of chairs facing the giant TV screen.

Still holding on to each other, they settled in front of the large shiny monster, still pumping out images of men in red shirts running and bumping into each other. All attempting to fight over a black and white ball, on the biggest lawn they'd ever seen. Billy, now satisfied that his two young guests were settled, deliberately rubbed both his thumbnails together, mumbling something to himself.

"Watch carefully, and believe all you see." Billy smiled at the two nervous twins. A recording of Liverpool's last home match against Arsenal slowly transformed into a stationary white fluffy cloud, completely covering the screen. Both the recording of the match and the commentary was now fully replaced by Billy's magical real-time 1192 AD images.

"Keep watching, nothing to be afraid of, my young friends!" Billy moved closer to the royal twins, easing between them.

Gradually, the cloudy mist cleared, and a familiar sight filled the giant screen. There, standing on the edge of the pine forest, Jed was on his knees, peering under the garbage cart. Whilst Seth was hurrying around, his face creased with anger. As the bird's eye view of the carter's search in 1192 AD for the royal twins continued, both could not be certain if this was a dream. As the action developed, Axle and Imogena began to see the funny side of the new images displayed on the magic mirror.

"Serves 'em right," Billy offered. "They're both your grandmother's spies. How they goin' to explain this away? But now you need to see more. I know he's waiting to know you're safe." Billy smiled at the twins, sensing that they were settling down, as they attempted to understand the fast moving events and how their world was changing. Billy understood the brain-boiling confusion which the twins were suffering. Smiling at the two royal children, he recalled the first time he'd slipped through time.

CHAPTER SIX

Young Billy meets his future
2006 AD
Liverpool

Gilmour Junior School, just off Duncombe Road – Billy's primary school – sat in the comfortable suburb of Garston, where a cross-section of scousers resided in tree-lined calm. As Billy entered his final year at primary school, his thirst for knowledge was swamped by a desire to taste the reality of medieval history. His form teacher, Mr Gerald, an aging bachelor with a permanent smile, was obsessed with running projects and special features on the Holy Wars. On several occasions, Mr Gerald arranged events mirroring specific battles, ensuring that he also indulged, by dressing the part as an English Crusader.

But unknown to Billy, Mr Gerald had discovered a special power which would allow him to make a permanent trip back to his beloved period of history. For once settled back at a spot in medieval history, there he would stay, there being no return to travel alternate Saturdays to watch his beloved Liverpool, swaying amongst his friends towards the back of the Kop. His current heroes – Stevie Gerrard, Jamie Carragher, Michael Owen – and his all time idols – Kenny Dalglish, Alan Hansen and Ray Clemence – were destined to become just happy memories.

Many afternoons, after school had closed for the day, and his friends had departed to play a five-a-side football match at Long Lane Rec, in the gathering winter gloom, Billy sat with Mr Gerald, exploring even more of his passion for medieval history. Mr Gerald collected history books from Garston Library, each to assist Billy's thirst for more in-depth knowledge of a bloody time in the country's history.

With his friends already long gone for the day, Billy settled down in Mr Gerald's tiny office with yet more books, awaiting his teacher's arrival. As the minutes ticked by, Billy began flicking through the piles of history and reference books which Mr Gerald had assembled. Under a pile of illustrated reference books, Billy became captivated by a grubby illustrated leather-bound tome. Its pages were yellowed by age, and some were torn by a history of thumbs rubbing over its delicate paper. Time slipped past for Billy as the winter evening darkness closed in. So engrossed by the content of the old leather volume was Billy that he was unaware of the fading light. But somehow, the old leather book had a mind of its own; its pages offered a tender glow, allowing Billy to continue flipping through its aging folios.

But what happened next changed the direction of Billy's life. Turning over the next page, the old book shook itself, forcing back the two halves, stopping any further progress. The book had decided that Billy should concentrate on the two open pages, aided by an increasing glow. Slowly, Billy worked his way through the Italic script and detailed drawings of the pages entitled – TIME TRAVEL.

"Welcome, Billy! I wondered how long it would be before you'd find me," the antique book delivered, in a soft, motherly voice. "Don't be frightened, Billy; yes, it's me, Astrid, talking to you, the crumbling old history book."

In shock, Billy let go of the book, uncertain what was happening, and scared at being spoken to by an inanimate object. But as he released both hands from the book, it defied gravity and just hovered, before changing from the horizontal to an almost vertical position. Its pages, which, earlier, had been lit by a soft amber glow, slowly turned to a much brighter shade of ivory.

"Don't go, Billy, Mr Gerald knows. We've both been waiting for many years for the right person to join our special clan. Billy, you see what I'm called? *Time Travel*. You're a very lucky boy, Billy, you're the special one. I suppose I should tell you about the others waiting for your help."

Billy slumped back against the wall, staring at the old history book, its pages glowing, as it defied gravity, suspended above him. There was nothing to fear as he watched the hypnotic glow emanating from the hovering tome which he had hoped would provide him with the medieval knowledge he craved. But perhaps this really was the history lesson he craved. But what Billy was soon to learn was that he was about to become part of medieval history.

CHAPTER SEVEN

Let the magic spells commence
2006 AD
Liverpool

"Ah, so you've found my old friend Astrid, I can see?" Mr Gerald brushed into the room, spotting Billy still squatting against the wall, spellbound by the hovering leather tome.

"We've found the one, Gerald; Billy is perfect, just as you suggested." The motherly voice filled the room, echoing around Mr Gerald's tiny office. "Now it's your time to move on, as we planned, Gerald," Astrid continued. "Shall I explain to Billy, or will you? No, I think it's better if I explain."

"If you don't believe in magic, Billy, then now's the time to start. Now that I've found you, your Mr Gerald can be sent on his mission. Not to watch his beloved Liverpool playing in Munich or Barcelona! No, my dear, he's going back to the Middle Ages – I know you prefer to call it Medieval Times – he'll be there to help you when you arrive. But here's the difference. When I send Gerald back, there's no return. But he will be able to talk with you across time. I know it's complicated."

Mr Gerald sat closer to Billy and squeezed his sweating hand. Billy looked up at his smiling face, still coming to terms with the magnitude of events unfolding. If Mr Gerald went back to the Medieval Times, would he ever see him again? But what could an eight-year-old boy from Garston do? Why was he being selected? And where was he destined to go?

Astrid's pages appeared to brighten even more, as both pages ruffled slightly. Two motifs on either page eased their way from the old leather book, suspended from the glowing pages. Both embossed images gradually changed shape. No longer were they flat, one-dimensional drawings of two oval seals, one covered with gold inscriptions, the other silver. As they floated from the pages they transformed into solid ovoid objects, both slowly rotating, displaying strange hieroglyphic engravings; each one slightly unlike the other.

Mr Gerald offered Billy his hand, lifting him upright, moving closer to the ovoid shapes, which were now radiating a glow similar to that of the two pages. As both Mr Gerald and Billy moved closer to the hovering "eggs", each one flew gently away from the old leather book, fastening to their respective right hands. Mr Gerald now held the golden ovoid, and Billy nervously clung to the silver egg.

"There we go!" Astrid joined in with the action. "They've made their choices: gold for a one-way journey, and silver to travel back and forth. Of course we all knew that that was ordained somewhere in my fading pages. Gerald, you know that you're off to help save Palogonia from Queen Ventenil. There you'll become tutor to the royal twins, Prince Axle and Princess Imogena. Look out for Martha, she'll form part of your story.

Billy, will join you when the twins are ten. Good fortune, Gerald."

Gerald's golden ovoid slipped from his hand and hovered close to the left hand page of the leather tome. Then, with a flicker of light, it disappeared into the page, reforming as a one dimensional engraved image.

"Now let's explain your task, young Billy." The volume of Astrid's voice increased, displaying an enhanced sense of urgency. "When the Royal twins are ten, they'll need help. Then you'll be eighteen, Billy. No need to worry: all will become clear. I've chosen the two men I've been seeking, good luck! Oh Billy, by the way: when the time's right, just rubbing your two thumb nails together is all you need – and, of course, a good heart."

Following the same procedure, the silver ovoid slipped from Billy's hand, dissolving itself back into the old leather-bound tome. With both ovoids now settled back within the two pages of Astrid's magic book, a white cloud enveloped the room. As the cloud cleared, there was no sign of Mr Gerald. Billy rubbed his eyes, failing to understand what had happened. All that remained of the old leather history book was a small covering of white dust on Mr Gerald's ink-stained desk.

"Who's in 'ere?" The school caretaker burst into the room. The only occupant was a slightly nervous Billy Chen, leaning against his teacher's desk, bewildered at his reason for being alone in school, long after his friends had left. "Clear off, kid, or I'll let the 'ead teacher know you've been 'ere. Go – now!"

CHAPTER EIGHT

The kids have gone!
1192 AD
The Kingdom of Palogonia

"What's all the fuss today, Gerald? Extra guards on the gates, and no one's allowed to leave the castle." Martha peered out from Gerald's quarters, from where he also taught the royal twins. Both portcullises, on the eastern entrance, and on the main southern gateway, had been closed by the swelling numbers of soldiers. On the lanes leading to the southern gate, chaos reigned. Heavily armed soldiers and formally dressed courtiers pushed and shoved their way in no understandable direction. Countless voices screamed orders, making little sense, as differing hordes shouted over each other. Workers from the village, allowed inside the castle to deliver produce, and those working in menial jobs, were segregated and lined against the stone walls. As Martha and Gerald looked down on the confusion, a cunning smile broke out from Gerald's wrinkled cheeks.

"Make way for her royal majesty," a senior officer screamed, pushing back the chaotic mob at the point of his sword. "Silence for her royal majesty!" He continued to battle against the increasing volume from frightened lookers-on.

"Someone amongst the treasonous peasants from the village has taken my grandchildren," Queen Ventenil, bedecked in her full regalia, screamed at the crowds, pointing in the direction of the petrified villagers lined against the walls. "I shall save the life of the person who informs me of the culprit. But I shall start executions in one hour. One person from each family; they will cease only when I get the truth. Do you understand, Captain?"

Her bowing Captain straightened up, holding his sword aloft, moving towards the cowering villagers. Many were already breaking down, begging for mercy. Those with children shoved them between themselves and the stone wall, for protection. As the Captain moved towards the first villager, kicking his way through the baskets of vegetables, several other soldiers drew their swords, moving forward to commence implementing the Queen'sorders.

Outside the great southern gate, shouts could be heard from Jed and Seth, as they vied with the panicking hordes to be heard by the soldiers guarding both sides of the gate. Eventually, they edged one of their great cart horses into the crowd, working their way little by little towards the gate. Whatever Jed and Seth were shouting was lost in the confusion. Inside the castle, Queen Ventenil, having spotted the two wildly gesturing carters, forced her troops towards the southern gate. Immediately, a pathway cleared respectfully before her. As she strode closer to the portcullis, the eruption of noise outside the portcullis decreased, fear now spreading amongst the gathered crowds. Jed jumped from the cart, which was now jammed against the wall leading to the secured gate. Through the lowered portcullis, he could see his angry Queen approaching, guarded by a number of heavily armed soldiers.

"Captain, stop the first execution. Let me see what these carter men are doing, locked outside." Queen Ventenil closed up to the portcullis. "Raise the portcullis! I need to speak to these men… NOW."

As the grinding of chains commenced to roll over the lifting wheels, slowly the giant portcullis edged its way upwards, exposing a clear entry into the castle. Jed stood in front of the massive black cart horse, ensuring that he blocked any possibility of the giant horse's moving towards his Queen. A roar of competing voices was hushed as Queen Ventenil moved within a few feet of Jed, who bowed, waiting for her permission to straighten upright.

"What do you have to tell me, carter?" Queen Ventenil placed her hand under Jed's chin, forcing it up, so that she could stare into his watering eyes. "Quickly, your life is mine to take, and the other carter's. Don't let him escape," she pointed towards Seth, already surrounded by castle guards, propelling him towards Jed.

"Yer majesty, we wus just returning to tell yuh about the twins, but we wus locked out," Jed visibly shaking, spluttered his words out. "'Im and me saw 'em near the big forest where we takes da rubbish, yer majesty. We tried to stop 'em when somethin' strange 'appened, yer majesty. There wus a great silver flash, which knocked us over, an' when we got up they wus gone. Right weren't it?" Jed prodded Seth, still bowing in the presence of his Queen.

"Captain, take them to my chambers. I'll get the truth from these vermin. Silver flash? Really," Queen Ventenil chuckled to herself. "You can stop the first executions until we've heard what these two have to say. I have ways, Captain."

Gerald and Martha eased back from their elevated viewing position, out of sight of the Queen and her entourage. Having watched the whole affair unfurl beneath them, Martha was even more uncertain what was happening. Gerald guided Martha back into his quarters, with a surprising spring in his step. Martha had rarely seen the old tutor so sprightly.

"Oh, Martha my dear girl, now I can reveal the truth to you. I've given you a wonderful education, and now it's time for you to use your understanding from much of what I've taught you. Martha, firstly, you now understand history from the books we've studied. But there's another dimension. The future, Martha! Not just ideas, and what we hope for, but a chance to visit there as well."

Martha eased back onto several cushions, sitting in a Yoga pose, saying nothing, just trusting, yet confused by the words coming from her dear learned friend.

"Martha, I came from the future around ten years ago, a few days after the twins were born. You will recall that we first met when you were around eight, I believe," Gerald hurried on with his startling explanation. "I was a teacher called Mr Gerald, for children up to eleven years, in the twenty-first century. I grew up in the northwest of the country, in a town called Liverpool. What's even more amazing is that I was sent here by an old book called Astrid, to save the twins and their mother, Princess Xena. Whatever you've heard, Martha, the Queen's only daughter is still alive. And maybe her husband Prince Gandolf is also alive," Gerald tried to continue, as Martha grabbed his arm.

"Gerald, I'm trying to understand what you've told me, but my brother, Jasper, is also still missing. Well, we've heard nothing for nearly three years." Martha started to shudder as emotions about her brother were relived.

"I understand, Martha, but there's more. I know where the twins are. No amount of searching in Palogonia will find them. I had them removed to safety, where they can start to search for their father. Once we've found him, the next stage is to release Princess Xena and remove Queen Ventenil from the throne."

Along the corridors which opened onto Gerald's quarters, competing voices increased in volume, making their way towards the Queen's chambers. A loud banging on Gerald's door stopped the intriguing story around which Martha was trying to twist her mind.

"Gerald, you're required in her majesty's chambers," an intense male voice shouted from the corridor. "Do you hear, Gerald? There's a major problem."

"I understand," Gerald called back, without opening the door. "We've just time, Martha; follow me to the classroom, my dear. I can see that you need to know more. Come!"

Gerald's classroom was probably the smartest, and, indeed, the largest room in his quarters of the vast west wing of the castle. Unlike other classrooms, it contained just three desks: two small desks for the royal twins, and another sprawling desk covered with Gerald's books and exam papers. A curved wall, mirroring the shape of the tower in which the classroom was set, was covered with maps and illuminated posters, explaining various periods of history. On the only straight piece of wall hung a large ornate mirror, bearing a number of crests of past royal family members.

"Sit here and watch, Martha, but what you see must remain a secret. Do you understand, my dear?" Gerald chuckled to himself, knowing that he was taking a eighteen year old girl into a magic circle which few would ever be privileged to enter. Gerald stood before the ornate mirror, now reflecting a perfect vision of the old tutor. His eyes now closed, Gerald carefully rubbed his thumb nails together, seeming also to mumble to himself.

As Gerald lowered his hands, a silvery cloud oozed from the old mirror, and then gradually faded away, leaving images slowly appearing into focus. The mirror was now filled with a young man dressed in clothing unlike anything she'd ever seen. His smile was dazzling; his slightly rounded handsome face caused Martha to glow inside.

"Gerald, you there, my man?" the handsome face spoke out from the mirror. "They're here and safe as we agreed. Quite the little scousers now, Gerald; Kop End next, I reckon."

As the handsome face began to talk to Gerald, the picture moved to the right hand of the young man. There, now bedecked as dedicated Liverpool supporters, stood Prince Axle and Princess Imogena, staring out from the twenty-first century.

CHAPTER NINE

Unlikely friends
1192 AD
Somewhere in the Holy Land

Prince Gandolf woke alone from a fitful sleep amongst a dense patch of bullrushes which sloped down towards the edge of the fast-flowing Euphrates. For nearly three years, Prince Gandolf had hidden from capture, dodging the Muslim enemy throughout the Great Seljuq Empire. In the midst of one blood-curdling battle, Prince Gandolf's small group of twenty-two well-armed soldiers had become separated from the main body of Christian Crusaders. But tragically, as the initial months passed by, first due to incurable sickness, and then to capture, he was left alone.

Since the loss of his fellow Crusaders, Gandolf had travelled alone for several years, considering that all hope of returning to the main Crusading armies was lost. Early one morning, as the sun rose over the distant mountain range, Gandolf cautiously approached the smouldering remains of a small village. Across the wreckage, white smoke drifted on the morning breeze, away from the war-damaged buildings. The only sounds wafting from the devastation were screams from a flock of scavenging peregrine falcons and golden eagles, fighting over the bodies of several dogs left by the departing rebels.

"Leave 'em, go, yuh beasts, GO!" A scrawny young man, dragging his left leg along, ran into the flock of scavengers, all determined to feast on the animal remains.

Gandolf watched as the young man fought vainly to shoo the mighty scavengers away from the carcasses. Try as he might to fend off the increasing number of birds of prey, eventually the crippled young man slumped down exhausted, leaving the food chain to follow nature's inevitable course.

For several years, as Gandolf had wandered across the endless deserts of the Holy Lands, he had treated everyone and every situation as his enemy. By adopting an over-cautious attitude, he had survived one day at a time, leaving him a possible chance of making his way home. From behind the remains of what appeared to be a family home, Gandolf watched the crippled young man. If he was the enemy, Gandolf was certain that he could overpower the stranger. For there were no weapons in sight. If a fight started, neither would have the advantage of a sword, nor any form of fearsome weapon. Also, the young man spoke English, albeit in an accent which he would expect from the peasants working on his father's land. Maybe this was the friend he needed, even though he seemed to be carrying a damaged leg.

"I'm a friend, young man, don't be afraid." Gandolf eased his way through the heaps of rubble towards the stranger, who was still staring at the screaming birds of prey. "I'm Prince Gandolf of Castonia, separated from the Crusade." Gandolf moved closer to the young man, extending both his hands in a gesture of welcome and peace.

"Jasper, Jasper Castleman my Lord." Jasper eased himself from the floor, accepting Gandolf's hands to stand in front of the stranger Prince. "I didn't run away, sir, I wus hit and left fer dead when the savages raided our food wagons. Lucky, I suppose; been wanderin', keeping just behind the savages. They usually leave somethin' I can feed on. Not like these poor devils." Jasper pulled Gandolf away from the screeching birds, and the sight of them driving their sharpened beaks into the slaughtered remains. "Sir, don't I know you? You're married to our Queen's daughter, aint yuh?

"Jasper, out here there's no Prince or serf; we've both got the same problem." Gandolf smiled at the first friend he'd met for several years, as he'd skipped from one danger to another.

Sometimes luck can be found in the strangest places. Two men from completely different cultures, thrown together by the side effects of war. Two men determined to return to their families, now with a common bond, but with widely differing outcomes on reachingPalogonia.

As they continued their travels together, both suffered illness brought about by unclean drinking water, and by inedible food scavenged from any source possible. But somehow, they'd survived. As the months slipped by, their body's tolerances compensated to match their limited diet. A resistance to the infrequent and often inedible food and unclean water which they managed to beg, borrow and steal, somehow assisted their survival. Furthermore, they had become adept at fishing, by standing for ages in the shallows of the Euphrates, mesmerising carp, and, occasionally, catfish. With the absence of fire, Jasper filleted their river catch, sometimes eaten raw or occasional he would cook their bounty in the blistering Arab sun.

Most of their survival techniques had been provided by Jasper. His late father had introduced Jasper and Martha to the ways of the countryside, navigating the vast uninviting forests, and utilising the great river Palo that crossed the kingdom of Palogonia. There was a dogged determination shown by Jasper, mostly as a result of his deformed lower left leg. Jasper was always determined to show that his physical derailment would never affect his qualities as a front line soldier. As Martha had initially hoped, when Jasper was initially conscripted into the Queen's army, he had been placed in the catering section. His task was to travel with the host of food carts, ensuring that, as the armies travelled towards the battlefields, the carts were permanently fully laden with sequestered food, taken from any source they passed.

If Jasper was skilled in the arts of survival, Gandolf had academic skills, which allowed the duo to benefit from his knowledge of navigating by the stars. They had again crossed the Euphrates several weeks earlier, and were now heading almost due west. Gandolf was certain that his course would eventually bring them to the relative safety of allies, doubling as local fishermen, on the Mediterranean coast near Beirut.

Even before they had crossed the Euphrates, they had stolen local Arab clothing. Their disguises were now worn with lengthy black beards, allowing both Crusaders to pass off as nomadic Arabs, and also allowing them to disappear amongst the hordes fleeing from the war-torn lands. Their only problem was Arabic. Both had picked up a few words, sufficient to meet and greet and quickly to move on, keeping their true identity hidden.

With the Euphrates now well behind them, for more than three months they travelled west, only by night, finding shelter during the day, and sleeping away from the raging sun. Moving from the flat lands through the mountainous region gave them further shelter, where water was occasionally to be found trickling down the hillsides. Gandolf and Jasper were not the only refugees fleeing the conflict as they moved closer to the coast. Silently, they shared the rough terrain, along with others seeking to make it to the relative safety of the Mediterranean. As they moved stealthily across the rugged pathways, both were still conscious that enemy spies could be hidden amongst other travellers whom they encountered. Playing dumb to hide their identity was the obvious ploy when joining up with other evacuees.

Early one morning, they were ravenously hungry and weak from a lack of water, as the sun appeared behind them in the eastern skies; through the morning haze, in the distance, the Mediterranean became visible across the flat desert plain. To allow them to reach the coast, they must cross a foreboding stretch of open desert, which could certainly expose them to potential enemies. As the sun rose higher, the fleeing Crusaders cowered behind a cluster of rocks, sheltered by several sprawling Cedars of Lebanon. Carefully they considered the risks: could they make it to the coast before the sun reached its zenith, or should they wait, and attempt the short trip in darkness? At first, the new sounds reaching them sent them deeper amongst the outcrop of rocks. Human voices could be heard closing in on them, accompanied by a snorting, grunting sound and the clanking of metal against metal.

"'Ey look! That's the sea! We've made it, Edgar, my friend." A strange English accent floated towards them. The grunting and clanking increased as it closed in on them.

"Can't be, yuh must 'ave sun stroke Edgar," another strange voice shouted out, mixed with the increasing grunting and snorting.

Confused by the sounds of unusual English voices, and what they now understood to be animals, Gandolf peeked from their hiding place. Passing within no more than twenty metres were two giant dromedary camels, laden with leather bags. Both were led by two men in full Bedouin dress. But they spoke in English, although in a dialect which Gandolf had never encountered. Could this be their escape route, their way to the great sea which they had been struggling forever to find?

"Jasper, did you hear? They spoke English! Not sure: they could be spies working for the Arabs. What do you think?" Gandolf kept low down in the cover, even more confused at the dilemma facing them.

"'Ey, you! We're friends; don't attack us." Jasper jumped off the rock cluster, and, without fear, limped across to the strangers, leading their heavily laden camels. "We need 'elp, my friend, and we've bin travellin' fer ages. Yuh got water... please?" Jasper stumbled towards the two men, tripping forward, landing with a crash, against one of the stranger's sandaled feet.

"Yuh English?" Edgar grabbed at Jasper as he smashed into the ground.

"Leave him, he's with me," Gandolf screamed out as he appeared from the rocks, before stumbling over, his weakened legs finally giving out, collapsing face down in the sand beside the other stranger.

CHAPTER TEN

Hello Billy Chen
2016 AD
Liverpool

Billy Chen was the product of his mother's mistaken short term romance. The man whom he understood to be his father, an alcoholic merchant seaman, never returned from a voyage to Tokyo, shortly after Billy's first birthday. Billy's Chinese mother, Wendy Chen, never once uttered his father's name to her son, preferring to wash any further connection with the man out of her life. Her only consideration was to ensure that Billy, her only child, had a happy childhood. Billy loved Gilmour Junior School, to which he eagerly skipped rapidly along from their house in Bathhouse Road each morning. Being half Chinese, Billy had inherited his mother's beautiful dark green eyes and her long jet black hair; also, his mother's passion for education, and, particularly, her love of ancient history.

His mother talked endlessly about her family's history in trouble-torn China, particularly at the hands of the ruthless Japanese armies. On two occasions, Wendy took Billy to meet with their extended family near Guangzhou in southern China. For as much as Billy found the history of his maternal ancestors interesting, his passion was the Middle Ages: British Medieval history. His favourite period was that of the Holy Wars and the Third Holy Crusade, led by King Richard I.

Billy was fortunate that, as his interest in the Crusades developed, his favourite teacher, Mr Gerald, had, likewise, a passion for the subject. Mr Gerald was not only happy to feed Billy's interest in the Crusades, but also relayed detailed stories of King Richard I – affectionately known as The Lionheart – and of his army's famous battles in the Holy Land. King Richard was determined to take the responsibility to remove Sultan Saladin from Jerusalem, following early failed attempts. But Mr Gerald went a stage further. During the long school holidays, Mr Gerald travelled around Europe, where re-enacted Crusader battles took place. Mr Gerald was always bedecked in superbly tailored costumes, as worn by his hero Richard The Lionheart.

The staff at Gilmour Junior School never understood the reasons why, in January 2007 AD, Mr Gerald failed to return to school after the Christmas and New Year break. The head teacher received a short e-mail which stated – *"Following my dreams to another world"*. But one pupil understood what *"another world"* could be. Billy Chen knew that his favourite teacher had accepted Astrid's invitation, and had gone on ahead to commence work on a task which the "lady of the book" had set out for him.

On leaving secondary school, Billy had had no interest in seeking a place at University. For Billy had developed highly advanced skills in designing computer games. Without realising his calling, Billy soon developed a market for his skills, writing software for his games and occasionally for others seeking his expertise, writing their intricate software programs. So Billy, working from his bedroom, retained a life away from others, whilst financially supporting his mother. Billy understood that Astrid had other plans, when, and only when, the timing was right.

Shortly before his nineteenth birthday, Billy decided to explain to his mother the events from ten years earlier, with Mr Gerald and his meeting with Astrid. His mother listened intently, as Billy rambled on, leading more deeply into the complicated possibilities which Astrid had explained regarding time travel.When he'd completed his story, Billy waited with bated breath for an explosion of anger, or even hilarious disbelief. But his mother just sat, nodding gently, a broad smile exposing her perfectly-shaped mouth. For what seemed an eternity, they looked at each other in silence. Eventually, his mother moved next to Billy and held both his hands, tiny teardrops slipping down her smooth flushed cheeks.

"Astrid, eh? I remember when I first saw that tatty old book. I suppose she did her party trick, hovering, with her glowing pages changing colours? Don't look so surprised, son, it's all been planned for you to join Gerald since way back," Billy's mother began her surprise delivery. "In fact Gerald and I thought you might want to follow our ancestors in China. But Gerald has a task for you. Let's see how you progress; maybe your old mum might want to travel, who knows."

"You mean you've known all along? And you can travel through time as well? This is crazy." Billy could now see the funny side of what was being exposed to him. He came from a time-travelling mother. His mother probably knew more of Gerald's plans. This was zany.

"Billy, when you travel back to meet with Gerald and his friends, however long you're gone, when you return to this time you'll have only missed a few seconds. Sounds strange, but that's how it is," his mother continued without hesitation.

"Friends? Which friends? You clearly know who I'm going to meet. And how will I know when the time's right?" Billy began pushing for answers.

"You'll know, Billy; Gerald will send a message." Wendy Chen smiled mischievously at her son. "There's a small part of history that needs righting my son. All will come clear."

CHAPTER ELEVEN

Twins hear the truth
2016 AD
Liverpool

"Come on kids, let's go and eat, then we'll go back to my place." Billy attempted to lead the two royal twins away from the Liverpool F.C. clubhouse, towards his black Mini Clubman parked in Walton Breck Road.

"Just a minute, don't you understand who we are?" Princess Imogena blocked Billy's path, standing firm, stretched to her full height. "This is all very strange. I demand to be taken to Gerald our tutor; he'll make everything right. Now take us to him immediately."

"Imo, you're really something, quite the fighter. Now listen carefully to me. First we'll eat, then we'll chat to Gerald. He's knows you're safe. Now be quiet and follow me – please! Kids, come on." Billy shrugged his shoulders and opened the doors of his Mini. "Now you coming or not. My car won't bite you. It's just a faster version than your horse and carriages, only we don't need to feed it oats to make it move. Now get in – PLEASE!"

Reluctantly, the twins slid into Billy's Mini, now even more confused at the strange mechanical beast speeding between weird high-rise buildings. Eventually the three arrived at Billy's house, having stopped *en route* to collect a Chinese takeaway; they were ready to be exposed to noodles and crispy duck for the first time. All the way from Anfield, the twins had whispered nervously to each other. Billy was now convinced that they were hatching yet another plan to escape. But this time, with an eight-hundred-year gap since their last attempt to break free, an extra complication was blocking their way.

"Welcome to our home, children, you're safe here, no one's going to harm you." Wendy Chen ushered the two children into the house. "Come with me, time to try food from my country, China. When you've eaten, Billy will let you speak to Gerald; I know he's waiting. Now come along, there's a first time for everything, my dears."

Three of the walls in Billy's room were dominated by TV screens. In fact, a bed, positioned against one wall, offered the only indication that anyone slept there. His room remained blacked out, to allow the best quality from the various screens. Since their arrival in the twenty-first century, the royal twins had slowly been acclimatising to the strange new world. Colourful clothing, large mirrors that showed pictures of distant lands, mechanical horses that sped along quicker than their bravest knights on their trusty steeds could even dream of. Everything was bigger, faster, with shapes they could not yet comprehend. But now, settled in Billy's room, they were lifted to yet another level. As they squatted on his bed, Billy fiddled with his keyboards, which in turn lit up two of the large wall screens.

"OK, guys you need more explanation as to why you're here. This is going to be difficult, and until you can accept what I'm about to show you, I'm sorry, but you can't go back to your time. No need to say anything, just watch," Billy lectured, hoping that he could deliver all he'd been expected to achieve.

Billy went through his time traveller's ritual, rubbing both his thumb nails together and mumbling at the screens. Almost immediately, two screens flashed into life. One screen showed the riotous scenes at the South Gate, as Jed and Seth were frog-marched away by a cluster of the Queen's guard. Pacing along behind the two prisoners was their grandmother, still resplendent in long flowing ermine robes, pointing and screaming at anyone hindering her way back to the sanctuary of her throne rooms.

"You see, guys, that's the way your grandmother treats everyone, as though they're her enemies and guilty of some major crime." Billy added his interpretation of the scenes being transmitted in real time from 1192 AD.

"And you're safe there, my children," Gerald's voice rumbled from the other screen, as he came into view, sitting at his paper-littered desk. "You're with my friends. Alex, Imogena: listen to what Billy is telling you, it's all the truth. You've now been sent more than eight hundred years into the future. But don't worry, you'll be back when Billy and I have fixed a few problems," Gerald continued, unabated.

Gerald reached across the table and eased Martha into view, nervously standing besides the old tutor, her long blond wavy hair flowing to her waist, a pretty girl resplendent in her flowing plain brown dress. Like the twins, Martha was puzzled by the magic pictures which Gerald had produced. But she was also intrigued by the handsome young man standing beside the royal twins.

"Billy, will you explain our mission? But first, Axle and Imogena, you must understand that your grandmother is a very wicked woman. Furthermore, your mother is alive, imprisoned somewhere within the castle. But there's more." Gerald settled back for Billy to begin his explanation.

Billy rifled through a drawer beneath his cluttered desk, and removed a blue file which he laid on the desk in front of him. As much as the twins and Martha needed explanations, and fast, the quiet composure that Billy was now radiating brought calmness into the visual transmissions.

"In this file I've written down everything which Gerald and our friend, Astrid, had expected me to explain to you, and the tasks which Astrid wants me to carry out. But forget the file, let me explain in my own words." Billy moved away from the desk, standing closer to the twins.

Gerald smiled to himself, knowing that together with Astrid they had chosen the right man to carry through the life-changing actions for the downtrodden people of Palogonia. No longer was he watching an inquisitive eight-year-old, bewitched by ancient history. His friend had transformed into a very fine young man, who had every chance to see through the wishes of the old lady living within the aging tome. Hopefully, he would alter the lives of thousands of downtrodden Palogonians.

"Children, there is some good news which you will find difficult to believe. Your mother Princess Xena is alive, although under a spell concocted by Gayla, an extremely dangerous old witch who lives in the castle. Your mother has been drugged so she has no knowledge of your existence. But there's more good news: your father is still alive, although still in extreme danger."

Billy was now on a roll, but he paused to adjust the programme on the first screen. Slowly the crowded scenes of the Queen and her guards shoving the two terrified cart drivers faded away. In its place, two heavily-laden camels came into view, led by two Bedouin tribesmen, struggling across the desert. Lying across the two camels' backs were the prone bodies of two bearded men, dressed in filthy Arab clothing, tied on securely to the labouring beasts.

"Your father is the man on the left hand camel and, Martha, on the other camel is your brother, Jasper. I know that this is impossible to put into words, but Gerald and I have been following them for several days. It took us a long time to track them down, but soon they'll be safe. Then we've got to set about getting them back to Palogonia."

Martha collapsed against Gerald, grabbing around the old man's neck for support. Instantly, she began shaking as an uncontrollable flood of tears began pumping down her dainty white cheeks. Back in Billy's room Axle and Imogena clung onto each other, unsure what emotions were now overpowering them. This was not a time to offer too many words. The images Billy had released had told the truth, if only the three young people living in differing time continuums would accept what they'd now seen and heard. But now was the start of the task which Billy knew would require all his cunning, with help from the old rascal, Gerald.

CHAPTER TWELVE

Capture can be painful
1192 AD
The Holy Lands

"Take it easy boys, nearly there, don't struggle. 'Ad to tie you on; you think we're goin' to carry yer fat butts all that way?" Osbert pulled on the camel's reins, causing it to kneel down on the hot glistening sand, washed by the incoming waves. As Osbert's camel lowered itself, the motion caused Gandolf to slide from the side of the beast, still bound to the strapping holding its load.

"The rope's burning into my back; for God's sake let me free!" Gandolf struggled to release himself, his legs now resting on the damp sand. As much as he wanted to play the "I'm a royal prince" game, Gandolf knew that nothing positive would be gained by exposing his true identity. Edgar's camel having now moved alongside, went through the same procedure, lowering itself into the soft white sands. His canvas binding, not so tight as Gandolf's, although still firmly secured, allowed Jasper to roll alongside and slightly away from the fly-ridden grunting beast.

"So what's yer story men, run away from yer comrades did we?" Osbert thrust his challenge at Gandolf and Jasper. "Tryin' to escape back to England? Desertin' King Richard? Well yer just what we needs. My friend an' me, well yuh see, we're soldiers of fortune, head-hunters, mercenaries, call us what yuh like; catching the runaways for a price, that's wot we do. Two young men like you can bring a sack of gold from yer king. But yuh know, there's an even better price for yuh both. Yeah, I thinks you'll be perfect to be crucified as an example by the Sultan. Yeah Edgar, I think these two are perfect fer Sheik Amir."

"That's fine with me, Osbert, so let's camp 'ere tonight then we can take 'em on the fishing boat in the morning," Edgar replied, tapping his friend on the back, excited by the prospect of turning in two runaway Crusaders to their friend Sheik Amir.

Both mercenaries strode along the beach towards a ramshackle hut, leaving Gandolf and Jasper still securely shackled to the two camels. Both were choking on the camel stench, bitten alive by flies, and devoid of shelter from the boiling midday sun.

Shortly after they'd escaped across the Euphrates, a decision had been made to hide their identities. One thing was certain: the price collected on a royal prince was sure to be high. Especially one who could be heir to the thrones of two kingdoms. Gandolf had never been known as anything but Prince, Your Highness, or sometimes just plain, Sir. But here was a situation that required humility and a loss of his royal identity. Like many royals, his name reflected an association with many of his ancestors. His full title, only used on formal occasions, being Prince Gandolf Bergin Rexton Mauricio Arthur. But he recalled that his elder sister always called him Arthur, which, in these dire circumstances, would work perfectly. Furthermore, someone of royal breeding would never mix or even communicate with the serfs of the villages. Now hiding from the constant threat of their pursuers or spies, Gandolf knew that he must break with tradition, and show a common allegiance with the young crippled soldier.

"Jasper, you OK?" Gandolf whispered, just loud enough to be heard above the restless grunting of the two camels, and the constant breaking of waves along the sandy shore.

"Arthur, it's all my fault, I shouldn't 'ave rushed from cover. Don't know what came over me. I'm really sorry." Jasper wriggled against his bindings, still unable to break free.

"Forget it. These are dangerous men, they'd rather kill us in front of the Arabs to show their loyalty than take a few coins. Yes my friend, these are truly treacherous men. We've got to find a way to delay them. Once we're on their fishing boat we're dead men. Now think, Jasper, we need all your cunning, all the life-saving tricks your father taught you." Gandolf rolled as far as he could away from the camel, still bound by several bindings, across his body and secured to both legs.

Along the beach, the two mercenaries looked on as a fishing boat drove its way on to the shore line. Initially unseen by Edgar and Osbert, it moored its timber frame, several feet out of the breaking waves. A young bearded Arab fishermen let down the ragged sail, and tossed a sack loaded with the day's catch onto the sand, before jumping from the ancient fishing boat.Unconcerned at any danger the Arab fisherman might cause them, Edgar and Osbert turned away, more interested in their forthcoming meal. If they had treated the appearance of the fisherman with more curiosity, they would have noticed a white cloud as the fisherman disappeared from the boiling sands.

CHAPTER THIRTEEN

Beware the creepy old witch!
1192 AD
The Kingdom of Palogonia.

The heavy oak door into Gerald's quarters crashed open against the inside wall, smashing two plaster-cast ornaments into a thousand pieces. Unconcerned at the damage caused by their arrival, three bodyguards ushered Queen Ventenil into Gerald's empty living area. In the adjoining classroom, Gerald's ornate mirror was still transmitting images from the future of Alex and Imogena; both absorbing the story which Billy was explaining to both sides of the transmission.

"What's that noise?" Martha moved towards the door back into Gerald's quarters.

"Billy, we'll speak later." Gerald rubbed his thumbnails together, turning the giant ornate mirror back to its normal reflective surface.

Before Martha could open the door, she crashed backwards, as the three guards pushed open the internal door, allowing the Queen to step over Martha and stride to face Gerald. Behind her, shuffling along like a pet dog rubbing her hands, was Gayla, the Queen's witch, her bloodshot eyes scouring the room.

"When I tell you to attend me in my quarters, you old fool, I expect you there at once. Do you hear me?" Queen Ventenil moved face to face with Gerald, who was trying to stop himself from laughing at the futility of her actions. "What's this child doing here? I suppose you're going to tell me that she's carrying out cleaning duties. Remove the child to the dungeons, and give her some of your medicine, witch. NOW, AND HURRY!" the raging monarch screamed at Gayla, her face glowing red with fury.

"She's only a child, and she helps me, your majesty. Please, not the dungeons," Gerald's initial amusement quickly turned to horror, knowing that, once in the dungeons, no one ever escaped. A painful and eventual death was the only certainty.

"My grandchildren are missing, tutor. I'm certain you already know? I would expect you to be offering help, not playing with that child. Now where are they, tutor? Left loose, they can only be a danger to my rule as Queen. Now find them, tutor, I need them locked up in the castle. DO YOU HEAR ME?"

As Martha tried to extricate herself from two of the guards, her struggles were met with even more force, causing her to scream with intense pain. But the worst was yet to come. With a wave of her twisted hand, Gayla blew clouds of bright red powder in Martha's face, causing her to collapse unconscious into the arms of one the Queen's guards. Gerald eased back away from Queen Ventenil, attempting to regain his composure, still reeling from the sight of Martha being dragged away to the dungeons.

"Your majesty, I plead with you, not the cleaner girl, she knows nothing. Of course I'll help look for the children, but keep that witch away from me," Gerald implored, knowing his appeal for Martha's release would fall on stony ground.

"GET MY CHILDREN, TUTOR, OR YOU AND THE MAID WILL DIE!" Queen Ventenil screamed into the face of the quivering tutor, who now understood that his plans might have backfired on him.

Gayla watched as the Queen, followed by her guards, one carrying Martha over his shoulder, left Gerald's quarters. Gerald continued his pleadings all the way to his front door, before the door was firmly slammed in his face.

"Now you can tell me the truth, fool." Gayla moved from the children's classroom, having studied everything of interest. "We both know you and the maid know where the children are, teacher man. I will make you tell me, but my way can be painful to you both. Shall we say by the morning?" As she approached the main door, the old witch turned back towards Gerald. "No, shall we say in two hours?"

With that she slammed the door, leaving Gerald counting the cost of the disappearance of the royal children. But on the oak table, Gayla had left a small gift for Gerald. His favourite pewter tankard was waiting, charged almost to the brim with the Queen's best honeymead. But the drink had been laced with a little present that would allow Gayla to search his quarters, as Gerald slept off the effects of his honey coated present.

Over eight hundred years in the future, Billy's TV screen continued to receive real-time pictures of events acted out in Gerald's classroom. For even under extreme pressure, Gerald had turned off pictures arriving from 2016 AD. But he'd cleverly left his ornate mirror transmitting pictures back to the future. Gerald's incoming images would spell out the truth to the royal twins, more than a million words could ever explain. The truth about their evil grandmother, giving factual confirmation of Billy and Gerald's account of her intentions, and the despicable actions she'd already carried out.

CHAPTER FOURTEEN

Time to start the rescue
2016 AD
Liverpool

"Turn the pictures off, Billy, the children have seen enough." Billy's mother strolled into the room, knowing the children would need all the support she could offer. "Billy, we have to release Gerald's friend, Martha, she'll be needed to get her brother and the children's father away from the Holy Wars."

With both screens now blank, Wendy understood that she was the motherly adult figure the twins sought right now: an understanding friend, to help them live with the experiences, and the complicated and startling information thrust upon them. They were moving into a new experience. No longer were their lives to remain cosseted away from the day-to-day pain and conflict that faced other children, back in Palogonia. Now the stark realities of a new life had to be faced.

"Any ideas, Wendy?" Billy addressed his mother in the way which both had decided, many years ago, suited their relationship.

"Surprise me, Billy, you're the one with the original ideas. But don't be long, think of Martha on her way to the dungeons." Wendy squeezed her son's arm, before leading the twins from Billy's room. Wendy knew that her son needed space, allowing him to think alone, with the aid of his array of complex computing equipment. But even though he was working at the cutting edge of high-tech computing, Billy was fully conscious of the constraints of the time-travel rules laid down by Astrid, Gerald – and now maybe even his mother.

Gerald must be his first point of contact. By now, from watching in real time, he knew that the Queen and her entourage would have left Gerald's quarters. Now was the time to visit Gerald and devise a plan to release Martha from the dungeons. Billy recognized that he had the benefit of the latest technology on his side, but just how to use it was uncertain. The sooner he could get to Gerald the better.

Both Gerald and Astrid had made clear several important factors about the time travelling skills with which Billy had been endowed. There would be no inanimate objects moved through time. In fact, when the royal twins had arrived, even their clothes mysteriously changed, to coincide with their arrival point in history. Both royal twins still looked every inch, die-hard Liverpool supporters. Billy couldn't wait to view his new clothing when he travelled back to join Gerald. Modern weaponry could immediately change the balance of power, in any conflict in which Billy might find himself embroiled. But Astrid had made it clear that nothing accompanying him through the time portal must change the course of history. But surely his actions could alter history. So what was so special this time?

Billy's most potent weapon would be his new found ability of physical movement through the time portal; also, his ability to choose differing arrival locations, anywhere in the past. Astrid had also made it very clear that Billy could never travel past the current time he lived in, into the future. Another benefit was explained to him: that if the correct procedures were followed, Billy would be able to transport a maximum of four people through the space continuum. But only if he accompanied them.

Removing Martha from the dungeons had to be his first challenge; but to find a way forward, he must talk to Gerald. It was now over an hour since they'd watched as Martha was carried away by the guards. At the same time, Queen Ventenil had left Gerald's quarters. Certain that the Queen's entourage had all left and were well out of earshot, Billy decided to call Gerald. Hopefully, they could then conceive a plan to rescue Martha from certain death. For death was a certainty, once plunged into the depths of the castle dungeons.

"Gerald, can you hear me?" Billy watched as Gerald's classroom came into view. The door through to his living area was still open, the Queen and her guards having left.

"Gerald, it's me, Billy," Billy called out again, but there was no reply. Not a sound.

This was very strange, for there was no reason for Gerald to leave his quarters. Furthermore, Billy fully expected to hear from his friend, who was now alone, after the invasion from Queen Ventenil. But nothing: not a sound or sight of anything, apart from long golden drapes flapping in the breeze created by the open living room windows.

"Let me be with Gerald at his point in time." Billy spelt out his requirements as he rubbed his thumbnails slowly together. A silvery cloud enveloped him as he sped through the time portal back to 1192 AD, spot on the mark, into Gerald's living quarters. In a flash, Billy, now dressed in a brown tunic and horsehair breeches, stood alone in Gerald's living room. But there was no sight anywhere of Gerald.

"Gerald, it's me, Billy, where are you?" Billy waited for any response, but there was nothing. Then he noticed another door at the far end of the main living room which was firmly closed. "You in there, Gerald?" Billy shouted from outside the door. Disregarding any reply, now anxious that he was getting no response, Billy shoved open the heavy oak door. There, prone on his unmade bed, Gerald was slumped across the covers, snorting like an over-fed beast.

"Gerald, for heaven's sake, there's no time for sleeping, Martha's in danger!" Billy made his way towards the aging tutor, kicking against a pewter tankard lying empty close to his bed. "GERALD!" Billy shouted in the old tutor's ear, "I need Martha to go with me and bring back Prince Gandolf and her brother. That's what Astrid wants, you know, Gerald. Oh for heaven's sake, if you can't help, I'll go back and ask Wendy for help."

Billy looked again at the tankard, which somehow looked extremely suspicious. He'd never seen Gerald drink before. Billy picked up the tankard and smelt it, instantly tossing it across the room. "You've been drugged, my friend, sleep well, I'll be back. I'm sure the twins can explain the way to the dungeons. But maybe there's another way."

Billy moved back into the living area for a further check of anything suspicious: then, with a quick rub of his thumbs, Billy disappeared back to the future. His exit left one spectator watching in disbelief from behind the swaying window drapes.

As the silvery cloud began to dissolve, Gayla eased from behind the golden drapes, shocked at the disappearance, into thin air, of the dark-haired young man.

"So that's how you do it: black magic! But fear not, I have even stronger magic. Just watch, the royal children will be mine," Gayla uttered to herself, moving to Gerald's bedroom to check on her new adversary. As the old witch entered his room, she smiled at the discarded pewter tankard which she'd left earlier, with honey mead and her special brew.

CHAPTER FIFTEEN

What's the truth?
1192 AD
The Holy Lands

Jed and Seth knelt in front of Queen Ventenil, who was seated at her throne, leaning aggressively forward towards the two carters. Their heads bowed, ensuring not to make eye-contact with her. They had never expected to cross the thresholds into the royal quarters, a place where only courtiers and royal staff entered. But here they were, held under suspicion of their involvement with the disappearance of Prince Axle and Princess Imogena, and being interrogated by the ultimate ruler of Palogonia: a woman with a proven reputation of intense ruthlessness towards anyone crossing her path.

"I'll ask you one more time. What have you done with my grandchildren, carters?" Queen Ventenil bellowed at the two petrified garbage men. "Maybe I should bring your children here and you can watch as I remove one finger at a time. Or maybe one arm, then one leg. What do you think?"

"Yer royal majesty, what we've told yuh is all we knows. There were a flash, and then they disappeared," Jed tried to reach out and touch the Queen, only to be instantly whipped across his back by one of the Queen's guards.

"Fetch their children. Now! We'll soon get the truth," Queen Ventenil shoved Seth, who tumbled backwards onto the red carpet leading up to the throne.

"Stop, stop!" Gayla screamed, pushing past armed guards at the arched main entrance into the throne room. "It's not them, your majesty," Gayla wrested herself free from guards, gouging two of them across the face with her talons. "Come with me, your majesty, and I'll explain everything."

"This had better be good, you old crone, or it's you who'll lose your fingers." Queen Ventenil made her way to an ante-room, followed by two personal guards and the hunched backed witch. "Keep those men there, I may not have finished with them yet," Queen Ventenil pointed at Jed and Seth, still kneeling by the throne, surrounded by the Queen's guards.

Queen Ventenil slammed the door to the ante-room, once Gayla had followed her in.

"This had better be good, you old fool, make it quick and good. I want no lies. Lies mean your head. Do you understand?" The Queen's face was now glowing with rage.

"Your majesty, they have disappeared, exactly as the carters told you. When you left the tutor's quarters, I knew something was wrong. So I hid, waiting to see what was really going on. Your majesty, first I heard, then I saw a black-haired young man appear in the mirror in the classroom. Then, shortly afterwards, the same young man appeared in a cloud, across the room from where I was hiding. Yes, your majesty, in a silver cloud. The young man found Gerald; you see, I'd put him under a spell. And then, your majesty, he said a few words and then there was another silver cloud and he disappeared. He told the tutor he'd be back to save the maid."

"But where are my grandchildren, you old fool? You've not told me anything yet," Queen Ventenil moved towards the old witch, grabbing her bedraggled long white hair. "I don't care if you see silver, white, even black clouds. WHERE ARE MY GRANDCHILDREN?"

"But your majesty, they're with the young man with the black hair. They've been taken to a place called Liverpool, in the future. Also, your majesty, I've just told you the young man's coming back to save the maid whom you've sent to the dungeons. Then the two of them are going to bring Prince Gandolf and her brother back from the Holy Land. Your majesty, it's all true. And before the tutor, Gerald, went to sleep under my spell, he told me enough for me to know he's involved. Your majesty, have I not always been your most dedicated servant? Have I not carried out your every wish?"

"I see. And if I believe you, what do you suggest I do next?" Queen Ventenil slumped back against a table, pushing it with a crash against the wall. "How do we get to my grandchildren, if they're somewhere in the future? Have you thought of that?"

"I have two ways, royal majesty. With my own spell, I'll make Gerald the tutor send me into the future, so that I can see the children. Once I've seen them, I shall return and wait for the young man to try and save the maid imprisoned in the dungeon. If you remember, your majesty, Princess Xena's spell can be broken if her husband's wedding band is placed in her left palm.

Then she will become Queen, and you will turn to dust, your majesty."

"What are you waiting for, you old crone, go and kill my son-in-law, and then kill the maid and her brother." Queen Ventenil brushed past Gayla and out into the throne room. "Release the carters, but send them to the dungeons for one night, so that they understand my powers. And my grandchildren, you old fool, I have no use for them. Do you understand?"

Queen Ventenil turned back to the old witch following dutifully behind. "And when you kill the maid, make sure you kill as painfully as you can, the man with the black hair. I want to hear them both scream for their treasonous acts as they die."

CHAPTER SIXTEEN

Wendy has a secret
2016 AD
Liverpool

Back at Billy's house, the twins had settled in with his mother, comfortable in front of the TV. Wendy explained the features of the remote control, as they surfed excitedly across dozens of channels. Like all children faced with a new challenge, their excitement bubbled over, as Wendy introduced them to the magic of computer games. Their first efforts involved trying to comprehend the complicated building games within *Minecraft*, and, initially, left them completely bewildered. Looking for something easier and with a little assistance from Wendy; they quickly settled on *Stick Tennis*. In no time, they mastered the techniques of two partner screen games.

Having arrived back from his unsuccessful visit to 1192 AD, posing as an Arab fisherman, Billy needed his mother's help. For something had gone badly wrong, after he had set foot on the burning Mediterranean sand. But good fortune had been on his side. A safety device, which he'd built into the time portal, had triggered an instant programme, sending him back to the future, arriving, humiliated, back in his room.

"Hey look at you guys, computer experts already!" Billy burst into the room. "Wendy, we've got a problem, someone's drugged Gerald. He was crashed out on his bed, snorting like a wounded buffalo. Oh, and next to the bed was a beer mug, which stank of poison. Who could have done that to Gerald? I mean, what's he done wrong?"

"That'll be Gayla, grandmother's old witch. She's always with grandmother. Really creepy old woman, with long white hair and nails like a bird's claw. Gerald, and Matilda, our singing teacher, always kept well out of her way. Oh, really creepy." For a few seconds, Axle took his eyes from the electronic tennis match which he was now well into with his sister.

"She frightened me one day, when I wanted to go into the east tower. She said that it was haunted and was not a place for young children," Imogena continued, staring into the screen, trying to make a winning smash, as she remembered a day when the old witch had scared her witless.

"Wendy, can we talk?" Billy gestured to his mother to leave the two children, both deeply engrossed in a new technological world, already dominating their lives. "You guys OK for a minute?" Billy attempted to communicate with the twins. Nothing. Already they had joined the twenty-first century, oblivious to a world outside iPads and laptops.

"Wendy, I think you know more than you're letting on." Billy challenged his mother, who was already relaxing on Billy's bed. "Astrid, come on Wendy? She seems to be the good power with whom we're somehow involved. Come on, mother, what do you and Gerald know, that I don't?" Billy turned away from his

75

mother, to adjust an incoming transmission. One screen was still showing the coast of the Mediterranean, with two prisoners lying close by two irritated camels. In the distance, the evening sun was just visible, as it began to sink in the western sky.

Billy turned back to his mother, "Wendy..." His mother was gone. Instead, on his bed was an old leather bound tome, its pages open at the pages headed TIME TRAVEL.

"Yes it's me Billy, Astrid, or your mother, or, if you prefer, Wendy Chen. Your choice. Of course Gerald knows and we were always going to tell you, at the appropriate time. But now the time is right, Billy Chen," Astrid's pages began to glow, as the old leather tome hovered above Billy's bed.

CHAPTER SEVENTEEN

Time is running out for two Crusaders
1192 AD
The Holy Land

As the evening sun began disappearing across the eastern Mediterranean, a chill was felt by Gandolf and Jasper on the exposed areas of their damaged skin. Since their capture by the mercenaries, they'd remained shackled to the bindings of the two stinking camels. As the hours sped by, their wounds began to sting even more. Along the beach, outside the ramshackle wooden building, a fire was visible, heating a large black pot, which steamed away in the diminishing light. One of the mercenaries prodded at the fire, in an attempt to keep the flames alive, preparing their evening meal. Neither Gandolf or Jasper had eaten for several days. Their last food had been two overripe coconuts that had fallen into the desert from a small outcrop of palm trees. How long the rotting coconuts had laid waiting for the two men to pass, was anyone's guess. But for certain, both fruits were on the cusp of permanently decomposing. But food was food. The risk from eating semi-decaying coconuts was worth the possible danger to their health.

As the mercenaries' pot began to bubble away, tempting smells began to waft along the short distance between the ramshackle hut and the captured Crusaders. Not only were the prisoners starving, but neither could remember the last time water had passed their lips. There had been no offer of water from either of the mercenaries, who'd shown no interest whatsoever in their state of health. Not the strongest young man, Jasper had drifted between consciousness and lapsing into a fitful sleep. Gandolf, the stronger of the two, possessed a steely determination to retain awareness of the likely actions certain to be delivered by the heartless mercenaries.

"Yuh better not die, soldier. Need yuh breathing when we parade yuh in front of the good Sheik. Oh yeah, yuh two's goin' to please our friend," Edgar moved close to Jasper, tipping water into his gasping mouth from a leather water sack. "Easy son, leave some fer the big feller, I need yuh both alive. S'pose you'd like some of our dinner, eh? Smells good I know. Yuh know, Osbert's a wonderful killer, but when it comes to food, he's a gentle giant." Edgar tugged the leather water sack from Jasper, as he sucked at the final drops. Satisfied that he'd passed over enough water to keep Jasper alive, he moved towards Gandolf.

"You'll never kill us, mercenary, it's you that should be concerned. You'll never get us to your friendly Arab, never! We're not deserters from the Holy Crusade, we're both loyal soldiers of King Richard. If we could return to his armies we would. Now kill us both, if you're brave enough," Gandolf kicked out as far as his bindings would reach, just missing the laughing mercenary, who, as an automatic act of defiance, splashed water across Gandolf's scarred legs.

"Don't worry, soldier boy, we'll keep yuh alive just long enough to watch Sheik Amir kill yuh himself. But who knows, he might just keep yer pretty young friend as a slave," Edgar swung the leather water sack, smashing Gandolf's head into the sand. Happy with the damage he'd caused in response to Gandolf's outburst, he swaggered back to the ramshackle hut, and the food boiling away in the blackened pot.

"Arthur, you OK?" Jasper tried to stretch up to peer over the camel attached to his friend. "You're right, your highness, we have to escape before they kill us."

From the other side of the snoring camel, Gandolf grunted as he struggled to sit up, dazed by the smashing blow to his head. Both were now suffering from bleeding sores on their arms and legs, as a result of the leather bindings burning into their sun-parched skin. But their greater concern, driving them both mad, was the continual infestation of sand flies, who sought pleasure from feasting on their bleeding flesh. Of course Jasper had the right idea. If there was a way, both the blood thirsty captors had to be stopped, or, if not, taken prisoner by friends. But there was no one in sight to help; even the fishermen allies, whom Gandolf had mentioned, were nowhere to be seen. Gandolf and Jasper must handle life or death decisions now facing them, all alone.

CHAPTER EIGHTEEN

Gayla on the edge
1192 AD
The Kingdom of Palogonia

Gayla's sleeping drug, which she'd added to the honey mead wine, would certainly knock out Gerald for at least two more hours: sufficient time for Gayla to have another sift through Gerald's quarters, before she administered a new potion. This time, her special powder would be blown into his face. Her potion would encourage a feeling of comfort to Gerald, creating a need to pass over his secrets. Maybe she would discover more of his relationship with the young man who'd appeared from within the silver cloud. Gayla herself was under pressure. Having told Queen Ventenil her version of where the royal twins were hidden, she must prove her theory correct, or suffer the inevitable punishment which the Queen would deliver. But as a curve ball, she'd told the Queen that her main concern was to ensure that, if Prince Gandolf was still alive, he would never return to Palogonia. For Gayla knew that she was the only person who could prevent interference from the long lost Prince.

Gerald hadn't moved. Even before the old witch had entered his sleeping quarters, a chorus of snorting and whistling from the drugged tutor could be heard, bellowing throughout his rooms. There was no time to waste, whatever information Gerald held; she had to extract it with the assistance of her truth powder. Since Gerald's arrival at the castle ten years ago, Gayla had never felt comfortable with the learned tutor, who had found immediate favour with Queen Ventenil. Gayla had used all her powers in an attempt to obtain a background on the Queen's new favourite. But whenever she had broached her suspicions with the Queen, her concerns had been brushed away as a further bout of jealousy.

Until Gerald had arrived, shortly after the twins had been born, totally out of the blue, Gayla had had the ear of the Queen. Any questionable matter would be discussed between the Queen and the old witch, frequently calling for Gayla's magic powers to intervene. So here was the opportunity to prove what she had been attempting to explain to her Queen for nearly ten years. She would prove that the white-haired tutor had magical powers; and, furthermore, that he was hell-bent on using them against the Queen and her grandchildren.

"Wake up, you old fool." Using all her strength, Gayla shoved in an attempt to rollover the grunting tutor, to enable his face to become clear from the sheets. All she needed was his face exposed from the bedding, to allow her to proceed with the next stage of her truth treatment. Now with a clear target, it was time to extract the information which would finish the old tutor and prove her worth to the kingdom of Palogonia. From inside a baggy pocket, she pulled a small canvas bag containing the next stage of her truth treatment. Gerald's nose twitched like a frisky young rabbit's, as the contents of the bag were sprinkled across his face: a substantial dosage was blown inside his nostrils, causing Gerald to sneeze violently. Within a few moments, his eyes glazed, and a frown crept across his face expressing alarm, as he struggled to sit up, then rested against the backboard of his bed.

"Listen to me, you old goat. I know you've captured the royal twins. Now I can kill you if I wish; right now I've got you totally under my power. Or I can let you live, if you tell me where the children are. I've seen the young man you called Billy. Yes, I was here and I saw him disappear as well. Now, all you do is to send me where Billy and the children are hidden; then, maybe, just maybe, you may be lucky and survive."

CHAPTER NINETEEN

Deep below the castle
1192 AD
Kingdom of Palogonia

Now fully conscious, Martha stumbled down into the dungeons, dragged as fast as her bruised legs would allow by two hunky prison guards. As they sunk lower into the hell hole, the stench of rotten food mingled with smells left by human waste was overpowering. Even the guards began choking as they neared the cell, destined for Martha. Each step further down into the dungeons brought Martha closer to the realisation that she would never return to the outside world. Stories abounded of the short life span which prisoners endured, once locked into the blackness of the prison's living hell. As they descended, the only light came from the occasional flaming torches held by iron frames, attached to the walls leading deeper into the dungeons. Every step lower down increased the fear of the unknown. Once locked away, food and drinking water would be practically non-existent, most only suitable for the plague of king-sized rats, that ran freely between the cells.

"'Ere yuh go, young miss. Enjoy yer stay," one of the guards laughed at Martha, as she attempted to block her way through the prison's open door. Her attempts to resist entry into the stinking blackness of the cell were futile, as the two guards shoved Martha into the uncertainty which she was entering.

"I'll show yuh what yuh've got in 'ere." The other guard removed one of the torches from the wall, shoving past Martha, providing a limited amount of flickering torchlight into the cell. Cowering in the corner were two bedraggled prisoners, bug-laden grey knotted hair hanging to their waist, both men covered by white straggling beards. As the light from the flames spread across their corner of the cell, both prisoners turned away from the guards, cowering deeper into the corner of the stinking hovel.

"See, yuh got company girl, they won't 'urt yuh," the guard holding the flame chuckled to himself, somehow enjoying the horrors now prepared for Martha.

"That's enough, she's seen all she needs, put the torch back, let's get out of 'ere," the other guard tugged at his friend, aiming him out of the cell. As they began to argue over the torch, it slipped between them, tumbling with a crash to the floor.

"Leave the torch on the floor, and stand very still!" A mysterious deep male voice echoed around the dungeons, its location uncertain, there being no indication of anyone else's being in the cells. "I said leave the torch. Martha, they won't hurt you, get the torch, quickly," the ghostly echoing voice continued.

Martha had nothing to lose; the voice could not be from the two old men. There must be someone else hiding close by, maybe someone to help her escape, but how? Climbing from her knees Martha eased her way towards the flaming torch, which was now equidistant between her and the two departing guards. Both were uneasy, due to the haunting voice which was still echoing around the walls of the blackened dungeon; she was uncertain whether to move towards the flickering torch.

"No yuh don't girl, stay where yuh are: clever, but not good enough to get yuh out of 'ere," the guard cautiously moved to regain control of the torch. But as he approached the flaming light, it slowly lifted itself from the floor, pointing its billowing flame into the face of both guards.

"She's a witch, come on, shut the door, let's get outta 'ere, I've seen enough, come on!" One of the guards stumbled through the door, dragging the other guard away from the suspended flaming torch, the cell door slamming closed with a deafening crash.

"Well, that was fun," Billy watched on his new computer game as the flame chased the fleeing guards up the stairs. On the other side of Billy's Apple iMac screen, a flaming spear crashed open the cell door, then flew past Martha, securing itself into the wall, lighting up the cell.

"Hi Martha, it's me Billy. Leave the door open for those two poor souls, I'll deal with them later. Now close your eyes, and come and join the game.

Billy was determined to try out his new App *Prison Break*, using time travel for the first time with third parties. The first effort had failed when he had tried to move himself into the Holy Land, landing by fishing boat nearby Gandolf and Jasper, on the Mediterranean coast. Realising that his game plan had back fired, he returned to his own time to re-group and workout where the mistakes lay. Although he'd arrived through time, the fishing boat disappeared as he tried out the game on his computer. But this time he was certain that he could transpose the parts of the dungeon game to bring Martha back to Liverpool in 2016 AD. Plus, he could have some fun chasing the guards, removing the danger from Martha.

On one screen in the fading light, Martha was assisting the two old bearded men from the cell, as the torch began to burn down. What else could be waiting in the dark for the three escapees was still off screen. Three rats, the size of cats, scampered across the screen, to be fended off by the two aged prisoners, kicking out at the scampering beasts. Each kick made against the danger elements cleared a path from the cell, and lit a way up the stairs to freedom. Up and up the two old men climbed. As they fought off other predators, their beards began to disappear and their hair shortened. Every success they achieved, with points scored as they climbed from the dungeon, they became younger, with their tatty clothes being replaced with fresh tunics. With a crash, they shoved open the main door at ground level, bursting into a sun-drenched day. On the score chart along the bottom of Billy's screen, both young men had now scored a maximum, allowing them ten free games, both now bedecked in white Crusader smocks decorated with a red cross.

As the two ex-prisoners celebrated their escape, and a maximum score, Martha appeared on the screen, followed by two more guards giving chase after her. Billy knew that this was time for his special trick, which must work. This would allow his second computer to join the game, against the prison guards who were in hot pursuit of Martha. After a few seconds using Bluetooth, the two computers spoke to each other, transferring Martha into 2016 AD, onto Otterspool Promenade on the south side of the River Mersey. *Prison Break* had passed the next stage of development. Also, it had brought forward Martha into the twenty-first century and had saved her from the inevitable death sentence which the dungeons would provide. But the future for the two guards was not so rosy, also dumped into the twenty-first century in pursuit of Martha, just a few hundred yards behind. On arrival, both guards were transformed into louse infested tramps, struggling to fight off the attentions of two snarling Pitbull Terriers and a huge sable German Shepherd.

Along the Promenade, as they did every morning, dozens of dog walkers filled the extensive parkland area. Most were chatting aimlessly away as their excited dogs chased around the far-reaching riverside leisure area. As the dog walkers, most deep in conversation, amused themselves with the latest gossip, a beautiful blond-haired girl, in tight blue jeans and a white denim jacket, wandered aimlessly past them. She was lost in a new country, hundreds of years away from the horrors she had just escaped.

CHAPTER TWENTY

Spinning in space
Between 1192 AD and 2016 AD

Completely under the spell of Gayla's latest drug, Gerald followed her through to his schoolroom. Since she'd blown her truth powder into Gerald's face, he'd woken from the induced sleep, his body again under Gayla's control. Her plan was simple, for she had made a promise to Queen Ventenil that she would take control of any events that could possibly remove her Queen from the throne. There was a cast-iron certainty that the twins would now be aware of the truth regarding their mother. But more importantly, Gayla was now also aware of Billy's and Gerald's plan to rescue Prince Gandolf from the Holy Land.

To carry out her promises, first she must experience time travel. She recalled, many years ago at wizard school having met Cedric, a charming old wizard of indeterminate age. Gayla could never understand the tales Cedric would tell, of his visits to a place where men flew like the birds, in large shiny machines; also, of other travels, when he had marched across Southern England with legions of Roman soldiers. Maybe they were dreams, maybe just embellished yarns; but each time Cedric told his time-travelling tales, something always stayed with Gayla. So maybe this was to be her chance to test whether Cedric's wonderfully colourful tales had any possibility of truth.

"Now listen to me, Gerald, my friend," Gayla began with a friendly approach. "This is what you're going to do. You're going to send me to visit your friend Billy, that young man with long black hair and green squinty eyes. There's no danger, Gerald, I just need to check that the royal twins are safe and well. Now let's get on with this, shall we?"

But safe and well was not on her agenda. The sooner both the royal twins and then Prince Gandolf were dead, the sooner she would again be Queen Ventenil's favourite and most trustworthy servant. Aware that she must remain proactive and be prepared to strike at the very first opportunity, Gayla had slid a short duelling sword beneath her cloak.

Gerald moved behind his desk, taking up his masterly position, as though waiting for his pupils to join the first lesson of the day. But although he looked scholarly, and in control, his actions were seemingly under the command of the devious old crone.

"I can't send you alone. Only those with the power can take you through time. I shall have to take you. Stand close to me, and hold my tunic." Gerald arose from his desk, moving close by the ornate mirror that had first introduced the mysteries of time travel to Martha and the royal twins. Gerald began rubbing his thumbnails, offering a short incantation, "Move us both to meet with Billy – move us now to where he sits."

Even for a witch with a reputation of delivering evil with no conscience as to the outcome, Gayla was entering a new field of unchartered magic. But even with the uncertainty of moving through time with Gerald, she was supremely confident that this would allow her to carry through the promise she'd made to her Queen.

Where Gerald and Gayla had stood a few seconds earlier, was just the hint of a white cloud, into which the two time travellers had disappeared. For even though Gerald had been drugged with Gayla's truth powder, just prior to performing his ritual to travel through time, he was practically back in control of his own body again. As he executed his time travel incantation and thumb-rubbing, Gerald smiled to himself, knowing the futility of this performance. When Astrid had selected his side of the old tome all those years ago, she was clear that once he'd travelled back to the Middle Ages, there he would stay. Unlike Billy, who would travel freely back and forth, with consummate ease, Gerald was locked in a fixed time continuum.

Alone in his bedroom, Billy worked away, making adjustments to *Prison Break*. His latest changes would include Pitbull Terriers and German Shepherds as an additional danger. As he strove to work out the next stage of the game, from behind him came a familiar rustling of pages. Astrid was active, lifting herself from his bed. As Astrid reached optimum hovering position, around table height, both Time Travel pages opened, displaying a bright yellow glow.

"Billy, we've got an interesting problem. You're being followed by Queen Ventenil's witch, Gayla. Remember, the old hag who had Martha removed to the dungeons?" Astrid advised, in her soft, controlled manner.

"So how?" Billy chimed in."Oh, don't tell me she's put some kind of spell on Gerald? Silly old fool, tempted by that tankard of honey mead, I suppose? But he can't travel back here, we all know that."

"We know, and Gerald knows as well, they're both spinning around somewhere out in the space continuum, with our time portal firmly locked to both of them. Not a problem for Gerald, but for the witch, I've got to send her back right now, or we might just change the course of history, before I'm ready. When she returns she'll remember what happened before she left the Middle Ages, but the travel and the return trip will be permanently blocked. Billy, you've got to dump her into one of your new App games. We need to control her now."

Gerald watched from a time lock, as Billy looked into Astrid's creased pages, as events unfurled. When Gerald triggered entry across a reverse time continuum, disallowed for him, it immediately set off a safety alarm for Astrid. Whatever magic Gayla attempted, Astrid had the antidote. Astrid would ensure that the old crone would never have access into 2016 AD, and the backstreets of Garston, within reach of the royal twins. The royal kids were safe, hiding with the time travellers inside the twenty-first century. But eventually, they must return to their own time. For there was a vital overriding factor that would permanently affect their lives. Travelling into the future, retaining their current physical format and age, could only last for seven days. Shortly afterwards, their bodies would quickly age, matching the actual time which they had reached. As they were currently over eight hundred years into the future, once the seven-day safety margin had been passed, their bodies would turn to dust.

"Billy, let's consider where we've reached. Both kids are safe, but they've got five days before they turn to dust. Gerald's safe once I send him back, but for sure the Queen and the old crone will remain suspicious that he's involved with the disappearance of the kids." Astrid calmly articulated the prevailing state of play. "I can only turn back the witch's memory so far. I'm sure she'll still be on Gerald's case when she finds out that Martha has escaped from the dungeons. It won't take her long to work out that Martha's with the kids. By the way, Billy, Martha's wandering around down by the Mersey. I suggest that Wendy collects her. Have her take the kids: that way Martha will begin to understand."

"Seems like we've got to finish the task and collect Gandolf and Jasper. I tried once, but the game failed. I think this time I'll whizz over to Beirut, that's if they're still held captive by those mercenaries. It's too dangerous to take Martha. She can wait here till I'm ready, then I'll..." Astrid cut off Billy's plans.

"No, no, she must come with you. Think it through, Billy – Martha comes with you and you move all three back to the castle before you trigger events to remove the Queen. It's got to be that way, Billy. Martha's a toughie and you need her help." Astrid moved closer to Billy, her soft voice hypnotic yet forceful, making sense regarding the next stage of Billy's adventures.

CHAPTER TWENTY-ONE

Return from the future
1192 AD
Kingdom of Palogonia

Gayla stood glaring into the large ornate mirror in Gerald's classroom, trying, for the moment, to comprehend the reason why she was transfixed in Gerald's quarters. Close by, seated at his desk, Gerald watched as Gayla regained her composure, after having been dumped back into her own time zone. Gerald understood that Astrid would have cleared the old crone's mind of the travel, both towards the twenty-first century, and back to the Middle Ages. But Gayla would still have memories of the black-haired young man who had appeared in a cloud of white vapour, and had then disappeared in the same way. Her suspicions would still remain, that Gerald was the main protagonist in the disappearance of the royal children.

"Can I help you, Gayla?" Gerald moved from behind his littered desk standing behind the old witch, both their images fully displayed in the ornate mirror.

A tension hung in the air between them, both uncertain exactly what the other knew. Gayla stood for a few more seconds, her brain spinning in an attempt to remember why she was standing transfixed in the tutor's classroom. Gerald, although aware of the safety measures taken by Astrid, knew that the crafty old crone would never let go until she had won her battle to ensure that Queen Ventenil remained in power. Without uttering a word, Gayla threw a distrustful glance at Gerald as she brushed against him, making her way to the main door of his quarters. Gerald slumped back in his chair, breathing heavily, knowing that this was the just the beginning of the fight to displace Queen Ventenil.

"I'm back, Billy; the old crone's gone, but she'll be back." Gerald peered into the ornate mirror at the moving image of Billy, with Wendy hovering in the background.

"Gerald, Martha's here, talking with the children. A little confused, but she's safe." Wendy moved to the centre of the screen. "Billy rescued her, using one of his new computer Apps. It doesn't matter; I'll explain later, it's a new-fangled gadget. Gerald, the plan is simple, Billy will take Martha back to meet up with Gandolf and Jasper, bring them back to you, and then you can install the real queen on the throne. You agree?"

"I'm not sure how to handle Gayla and the Queen. All I can do is keep my head down and plead ignorance." Gerald crossed to the entry door to his quarters, sliding two bolts across, securely locking the heavy oak door; and, hopefully, keeping trouble on the far side.

CHAPTER TWENTY-TWO

A pack of lies
1192 AD
The Kingdom of Palogonia

"Your majesty, I know where your grandchildren are." Gayla forcibly pushed her way past the Queen's courtiers, each attempting to find a place of importance close to the ruler. As Gayla made her way through the throng of hangers-on, many of the courtiers edged away from the Queen's favoured witch. Many had tasted the deadly actions which the heartless old crone could deliver.

"Let the old fool through to me." Queen Ventenil shoved aside two courtiers who were both attempting to make their presence noticed, armed with reams of parchment paper. Amongst the confusion of parchment and heaving bodies, reams of government papers were scattered across the red carpet leading to the throne. "Come with me, old fool, it had better be worth the wait."

Again Gayla was forced to follow a furious queen to the nearby ante-room, hurried along by three of the royal guards.

"So what news, witch? Speak and make sure it's the truth, and good news." Queen Ventenil grabbed Gayla's cloak, forcing her to her knees. "Guard, stand by to remove her head. The truth, old fool. NOW."

There was no point again trying to convince the Queen of her previous story. Queen Ventenil had already dismissed Gayla's explanation that her grandchildren had been taken to a country somewhere in the future. Also, her story of the black-haired young man's disappearance in a cloud of dust must be forgotten. Her new story must stay within the realms of credibility, even though it would be mostly fictional. But even if her new story was believed, she had already promised the Queen to rid her of Prince Axle and Princess Imogena. But the bigger threat for the Queen's remaining in power was to ensure that, if Prince Gandolf was indeed alive, he never made it back to Palogonia.

"Your majesty, your grandchildren are being held by a young prince called Billy in the Kingdom of Castonia. You may remember that, several years ago, I told you not to trust King Alfred. But I have plans, your majesty. My spies tell me that Prince Billy is to bring your son-in-law Prince Gandolf here, in an attempt to take over your throne. I have plans to kill Prince Gandolf and capture Prince Billy, ransoming him for the return of your grandchildren. Then, with your permission, your majesty, your grandchildren shall meet with a fatal accident."

Gayla turned her face away from the Queen, waiting for the swish of a cold steel blade as it severed her head, for failing in her duties and offering a story which the Queen didn't swallow. But there was nothing. Queen Ventenil made her way across the room, facing away from Gayla and the three guards. For what seemed an eternity silence reigned, as Queen Ventenil mulled over the new story which Gayla had delivered. Queen Ventenil eventually turned and walked slowly back to Gayla and the guards waiting for her reaction.

"Go: leave us!" the Queen screamed at the three guards, her mood having marginally calmed from her earlier actions. "Can you achieve what you say? I've not trusted King Alfred for many years. Why has King Alfred become involved?" Queen Ventenil pondered for a moment, for if this were true, a state of war between the two kingdoms should be declared.

"But this may just play into my hands," the Queen recovered her thoughts. "Go, do what you have to, and, once my grandchildren have been killed, then make sure that this new prince – Prince Billy, did you say? I want his head delivered to his father, spiked on a larch pole, with his face covered with mess from the pig pens."

Gayla bowed and remained bent low until the Queen had left and returned to the fussing courtiers buzzing around her, as she made her way back to the throne. Gayla had created a story that now required the death of the children and Prince Gandolf. Of course, as a bonus she would try to deliver the young Billy's head, but he would be forgotten once the throne was safe from internal claims. But first she must remove Martha from the dungeons and use her as ransom bait. Then her plans would commence. No longer would she adopt a pro-active policy against Billy, Gerald and whoever else was involved. She would wait for their arrival within the castle, and then exterminate the royal children, Prince Gandolf and Billy, at the same time. But what of Gerald? She was positive that Gerald was the ring leader of the plot to remove Queen Ventenil from the throne. For now was the time to breakout her very best spells. If she was dealing with Gerald and Billy, and maybe others with magic that allowed them to move through time, she must fight fire with even worse fire.

"Bring me the cleaner girl!" Gayla burst into the room occupied by five soldiers guarding the entrance to the dungeons. "I need her now, bring her to my rooms; but make sure she's been thoroughly scrubbed. I don't want to smell the filth from the prison. You understand?"

The senior guard jumped to attention, gesturing the others to follow. "Ma'am, don't yuh know? The cleaner girl, Martha, escaped. Very strange, the guards ran out reckonin' they were chased by someone throwin' fire at 'em. Two old men who we thought were dead, 'ave gone. No one will go down there; everyone says it's haunted, and fiery demons are burning anyone who enters through the prison door."

"You're all mad, move out the way, let me look." Without heeding further warnings from the guards, Gayla unlocked the metal-reinforced door and clattered her way slowly down the stone steps leading into the dungeon. As the light rapidly faded, Gayla withdrew her wand and relit the first torch, still attached to the wall frame. Dead ahead, at the bottom of the stairs, the door to the cell that had been home to the two old men, stood wide open. As she eased into the cell, a rustle from hundreds of feet, caused by a frightened colony of rats, scampered past her through the cell doorway.

A strange silence descended over the cell, with the plague of rats having left for safer ground. Gayla stood watching in awe, as the flame reflected against the empty cell wall, and a series of strange drawings. There was nothing. Apart from a few scratched etchings, not a sign existed that anyone had ever been incarcerated in the hell hole. Gayla shook her head, now fully convinced that the three prisoners had outside assistance. Not human assistance, risking life and limb to force their way past the highly-trained guards. No, this was certainly Gerald and Billy behind Martha's disappearance. If so, then Martha would certainly be hiding with the royal twins, somewhere in the future.

CHAPTER TWENTY-THREE

Time to search in The Holy Land
2016 AD
Liverpool

Billy peeped through into the living room, its walls flickering with a blue-tinted light transmitted from their 48" Panasonic TV, which dominated one wall. Sofa-bound, three refugees from 1192 AD chuckled with excitement, captivated by the sights and sounds radiating from *Madagascar*. Events which they had left way back in Palogonia, in another time, were lost for the moment. Like children from the twenty-first century, Billy watched in awe as Axle, Imogena and Martha lived every moment as *Alex, Marty, Melman and Gloria*, encased in wooden cartons, rolled from the freighter into the Indian Ocean.

Now was not the time to begin discussions of the next stage of the plans, agreed with Gerald and Wendy, from the instructions laid down by Astrid. For Astrid, as gentle as her delivery could be, was starting to push forward her plans to complete the mission in Palogonia and the Holy Lands. Billy's first attempt at bringing together a time move linked to his computer App, to join up with Gandolf and Jasper, had failed. But since his abortive effort, he had achieved success in moving Martha from the dungeons. But two guards chasing after Martha received much rougher treatment, having piled headlong into a group of dog walkers alongside the Mersey earlier in the day. But if his next time portal move was to be successful, Billy would need to bring three time passengers along on his planned rescue attempt.

Bringing Martha along on his rescue mission seemed to him to add danger to a plan already fraught with peril. But Astrid was the boss. It was difficult to argue with her logic. He would explain his plan to Martha, although he knew it was difficult for her to accept the magical side of his plan. There was a further matter to consider – the seven day time frame. Explaining Astrid's time travel conditions would be just too much information for Martha to comprehend, although, left alone with the twins, she was beginning to understand that what had happened was not a dream, although it was somewhat unreal.

Feedback supplied via Astrid suggested that Gandolf and Jasper were still prisoners of the two mercenaries, a short distance along the coast from Beirut. But even when he located the captives, there was the problem of how to extricate them from the mercenaries. The twenty-first century offered a myriad of possibilities how to overpower them, releasing Gandolf and Jasper. But the strict rules laid down by Astrid were cast in stone. Only flesh and blood could be transported across time, through the time portals.

That was it, flesh and blood. Dogs were flesh and blood, albeit not human flesh and blood. Surely, the dogs who, this morning, had scared off the tramps, would love a trip to the

Mediterranean seaside? And according to Astrid, travelling back in time held no dangers, as did moving forward in time; but only travelling to the place in time you had started from. Taking the dogs on an adventure away from their owners would not cause any issue. For on their return to 2016 AD, safely back to their owners, they would only have been missing for a few seconds. Not for the days for which they might be involved on Billy's mission, on the other side.

There was no point in explaining the rescue mission to Martha. Once the three dogs were captured within his latest App, he would find a way to move everyone back to 1192AD, on the shore close by Gandolf and Jasper: close enough to be within sight of the captives, but away from the sight lines of the two mercenaries.

CHAPTER TWENTY-FOUR

Let's get 'em Martha
1192 AD
The Holy Land

As the morning sun attempted to appear over the distant mountain range, a young couple in flowing white robes eased their fishing sail boat on to the sloping sandy beach. As the craft crunched to a halt, both sailors leapt ashore, hurriedly followed by two Pitbull Terriers and a massive German Shepherd, eager to have left the rolling deck of the tiny fishing boat. Excited to be back on mother earth, all three of the fisherman's pets rolled over and over in the searing white sand. Each one released its pent-up feelings, now away from the uncomfortable movement of the tiny boat.

Billy had hoped to land before the sun reached its zenith, arriving on shore with Martha and their attack force, with surprise on his side. But two elements had acted against his plans. Firstly, his navigation was somewhat awry, landing them between the mercenary's camp and the snoozing camels, which remained bound tightly to Gandolf and Jasper. If their landing spot was not a big enough issue to contend with, Billy had not reckoned on the excited yapping of his three dogs on touching dry land. These would certainly not be the only feral dogs roaming the shoreline. Billy could only hope to continue their surprise arrival, if his three dogs might encourage others to join in the barking chorus. Maybe a joint symphony of excitable dogs might remove suspicion of the new arrivals, mistakenly landing close by the mercenary camp.

"Let's get ropes on the dogs, Martha, before the mercenaries wake and spot us," Billy shared out several lengths of rope. "Quickly, towards those camels down the beach, now hurry. Aim for the trees!" Billy dragged the two Pitbull Terriers, handing control of the German Shepherd to Martha. Assuming this was another game, all three dogs accelerated along the beach; Billy and Martha were dragged along in their wake. As they sped away from their abandoned fishing boat, towards the camels, their path was partially hidden by the boat's sail which they had left erect. All along the sea-front, a thicket of palm trees offered shade and potential cover. Attracted by the sight of so many trees, Billy and Martha were tugged by the dogs towards the safety of the increasing number of palm trees, as they made their way towards Gandolf and Jasper.

"Jasper, doyuh hear that, wake up, sounds like wild dogs heading our way." Gandolf struggled against his bonding for a better view of potential danger heading through the misty morning light.

"Yeah, big man, wild dogs are always hungry. Still don't want 'em eating my prisoners do we?" Osbert appeared from behind the camels and tugged on Gandolf's bindings, ensuring that he caused the maximum pain possible. "Don't know who yuh are, but any closer and da big man won't need feeding. Yuh understand?" Osbert screamed towards Billy and Martha, as he dragged Gandolf back towards the snorting camel. Agitated by the commotion, one of the camels began to stand up forcing the binding to pull even tighter around Gandolf's wounded limbs.

Next to the deserted fishing boat, Edgar edged his way towards Billy, Martha and the three dogs, all now pincered between the two mercenaries. "Stay where you are, come out from the trees, there's no escape, we've got yuh," Edgar screamed, as he moved away from the breaking waves towards the line of palm trees, edging the shore. "It'll be easier if yuh show yerself."

"I'm 'ere Edgar, watch out fer the dogs, we got em," Osbert hollered out, as he moved away from the restless camels, each of whose movements strained the blood soaked bonds holding their Crusader prisoners.

Aided by the rising sun and the surprise pincer movement gaining them territorial advantage, Edgar and Osbert closed in on two sides of the clump of palm trees, hiding Billy and Martha. There being nowhere for the intruders and their dogs to run. But there was no one, no intruders, no dogs. Even in the improving light, not a soul was to be found amongst the palm trees. The only visual evidence was three dogs disappearing into the distance, striding towards a feral pack of hounds, further amongst the dunes.

2016 AD

Billy and Martha stood watching one of his screens, as events unfolded on the beach outside Beirut in 1192 AD. Billy was seething with anger that his second effort to rescue the trapped Crusaders had failed. He'd tried approaching the problem via an App game and this time as a straight forward time shift. But both had failed. Time was running out if he was to beat the seven-day cut-off. Failing that, three innocent people from Palogonia would become time dust.

CHAPTER TWENTY-FIVE

Time to attack the time travellers
1192 AD
The Kingdom of Palogonia

Now that Martha had somehow escaped from the dungeons, one of Gayla's bargaining tools had slipped away. Once the Queen became aware of Martha's disappearance, Gayla's neck would soon feel the power of cold steel. Gayla knew that the story which she had spun Queen Ventenil would not stand any truth testing. King Alfred did indeed have two sons, but the younger son, William, died shortly after his second birthday. Furthermore, King Alfred despised all that Queen Ventenil stood for, and would take pleasure in severing all connection with Palogonia, even without his son Gandolf in a possession of power.

As Gayla sat amongst the shadows of her cluttered rooms, she pondered how she could turn the current situation to her advantage. Martha was certainly with the time traveller Billy, somewhere in the future, definitely with the twins. As yet, she had seen nothing to prove that Prince Gandolf was still alive. But Gayla had listened intently as Billy talked about Gandolf, and returning him back to Palogonia. So she was definitely on the right track, but now with Martha elsewhere. The obvious was staring smack in her face – Gerald! Of course he was her pawn, her bargaining chip. This time she would make it known to Billy, and whoever was working with him, that Gerald's life was under her control.

Gayla snuck her way along the back corridors, away from the Queen's quarters and the prying eyes of those wishing ill to her. If she encountered a problem, a quick sniff of her white sleeping powder would remove any meeting from any potential intruder's memory. Gradually, Gayla made her way towards the distant wing of the castle, where the old tutor lived. Once she had made it there, entry would be no problem. If the old tutor refused to open the main door into his quarters, she would then resort to just a little magic: transporting herself as a cloud of smoke under the oak door. But first she must try persuasion. Gerald was a man who always sought a compromise, heeding the possibility of confrontation. But now the game had moved on, and she was convinced, now that he'd recovered from the two spells she'd administered to him, that he would be far more cautious toward her.

Gayla stood outside Gerald's door, convinced that she'd made it across the castle from her rooms without being spotted. All the possibilities which she could now use to complete the promise which she'd sworn to the Queen buzzed through her evil mind. For now, it was success in ridding Palogonia of the royal twins and Prince Gandolf that she urgently sought. If not, the end of the road for her as Queen Ventenil's favourite witch was a certainty. Queen Ventenil possessed an extremely short fuse and decisions were made instantly. There would be no second chance for Gayla. Indeed, failure in her mission to kill Gandolf and his children would probably mean the end of Queen Ventenil. Still pondering her next move, on further reflection, she decided that surprise was the only option. She would enter as a cloud of smoke, then returning to her physical form when she had understood more of Gerald's plans.

Gerald moved in front of the ornate mirror, preparing to communicate with the future. Having completed the procedures to make contact with Billy, Gerald waited for the mirror to receive pictures from the future. Slowly the misty cloud dissolved, leaving the mirror showing a clear image of Billy and a confused Martha.

"I'm in danger, Billy, the old witch is brewing up something nasty, I can feel it," Gerald spurted out, obviously now deeply concerned at the dangers closing in on him.

"Gerald, we're doing all we can. Martha and I have just come back from the Holy Lands, but we had to escape before the two mercenaries caught us. You know the rules, Gerald, I can't use weapons. If only I could." Billy stared back at Gerald, knowing that he wanted to hear something more positive.

"You're not giving up, Billy? We've got to bring Gandolf and Jasper back. That's the only way we can rid this country of the terror we live with," Gerald offered, his face wrinkled with concern.

A stream of white smoke slid silently under the door, connecting the school room with Gerald's quarters. When the cloud was fully assembled on the school room side of the door, it rose from the floor, transforming itself into the physical form of Gerald's arch-enemy.

"My God, behind you, Gerald!" Billy screamed out.

"It's Gayla! Gerald get out of there, she'll kill you," Martha burst on the screen, shoving Billy to one side, in an attempt to expose the dangers now surrounding Gerald.

Gayla stood behind Gerald, chuckling to herself as the reactions from the future were played out on the mirror. In 2016 AD, panic had set in as Billy and Martha, now joined by Wendy, watched, as Gayla stood way back in the Middle Ages, in total control of Gerald.

"At last we meet, Mr Billy," Gayla eased Gerald to one side, smirking into the ornate mirror. "As you can see, I can arrive at any time through any wall. Now, Mr Billy please don't think that you're going to bring Prince Gandolf here, that's if he's alive." Gayla turned to Gerald, tugging him with almost supernatural power back to join her in the transmitted images. "Mr Billy, I have your old friend Gerald under my control. You may think that he is under some magic spell, maybe, but he's mine and mine to control. By that Mr Billy, you must understand I mean to control whether he lives or dies. Is that clear?"

Wendy moved just out of picture, easing her way to the keyboard controlling the transmission, turning off the two-way sound.

"Billy, Martha, play her game, agree to whatever she tells you. Don't worry, Astrid has the answer." Just as subtly, Wendy turned the sound track on again.

"Before I tell you of my terms to save this worthless individual's life, I need to see the children. Don't even try – 'They're not here' – bring them to the mirror, NOW!" Gayla shoved Gerald onto the floor, her actions shown in every detail to the concerned viewers in Liverpool. "Hurry, my patience is running out. Be assured that I can drum up wonderful ways for the teacher to die."

Nervously, Axle and Imogena, holding on to Wendy made their way into Billy's room, moving even more cautiously in front of the giant screen affixed to Billy's bedroom wall.

"Ah, my children, interesting clothing. Don't worry I'll soon have you changed ready to meet grandmother. She's missing you so much, worried sick she is. Now listen, you'll soon be home, away from these evil people." Gayla's insincere smile glared out from the screen, causing the twins to hold each other, protecting themselves from the old witch's evil intent.

Gayla could now see that she had been right all along. Billy and his friends did have the twins. Once they were back with her, they would be the first to die. Gerald would watch, and then she had a wonderfully painful way to remove the teacher from her life. Then, plan two: to destroy any possibility of Prince Gandolf's returning to Palogonia.

"I'll be generous, Mr Billy, shall we say one hour to have the youngsters back with me?" The evil in Gayla's smile brought shudders to all who were watching her performance from their relative safety across the time continuum.

CHAPTER TWENTY-SIX

Move and countermove
2016 AD
Liverpool

His room now empty, Billy sat alone, pondering his next course of action. Twice he'd attempted to rescue Gandolf and Jasper. His first attempt had been foiled by his defunct computer game, which, for some reason, decided to return him back from the Holy Wars, defying the controls which Billy had created. His second effort, this time using only his time-travel abilities, had been aborted when the mercenaries guarding Gandolf and Jasper had out-manoeuvred both him and Martha. But now strict time constraints were his main consideration, if Gerald was to be removed from the clutches of the merciless old crone. His face to face confrontation with Gayla had brought the reality of the situation home to him. Time was definitely now his enemy. Maybe a change of direction regarding his attack was the approach. Maybe it was time to introduce his secret weapon, enabling him to create a double-headed attack plan.

Billy frequently worked late into the night on his new games. Some were for his own use, but an increasing number of software projects were for others who were keen to use his special software talents. Every night Wendy looked in on her son, suggesting that midnight should be the cut-off time for him to call it a day. But this night, Wendy had now already visited three times. On each occasion, Billy had agreed to call it a day. On her fourth visit, Wendy eased back the curtains letting in the morning light. Billy had not made it to bed, working through the night on his latest App game, *Time Crusaders*.

"I've got it, Wendy, this'll do the trick; but I need your support. You're the time traveller I came from: well, this is your time to show me how it's done." Billy slowly rose from his chair, stretching his cramped limbs.

"I thought you'd never ask me. So what's the plan, shall we discuss it with Astrid?" Wendy moved towards Billy's bed, where Astrid had last appeared. "The old girl always has the answer."

CHAPTER TWENTY-SEVEN

Time to move Gerald
1192 AD
The Kingdom of Palogonia

Wendy pondered exactly when she had last travelled through time. It had definitely been before Billy was born, when she had been forced back to Hong Kong, to extract her brother Jonny from a stupid conflict with the Triads. Jonny, always on the lookout for a 'quick buck' had crossed one of the main Triad families, when he attempted to sell them a collection of necklaces which he'd claimed to have bought from a dealer in Macau. Wendy really didn't care whether the jewellery was stolen or not. But she knew the Triads would ensure that her brother never escaped from a sealed rice bag, dumped way out in the South China Sea. There was little time to reflect on her past time travel, although she was certain that her brother had learned his lesson, now living a quiet life with his new family on the southern outskirts of Chicago.

Arriving back in time with Gerald, she would have all but a few minutes to remove him from Gayla's clutches. Once safely in Gerald's quarters, she must move rapidly to carry out the next stage of Billy's ingenious plan; in Palogonia, in 1192 AD, her only weapon was time travel. Gayla held the majority of tricks, most being laced with magic that could end in death. For this was war. The old crone would now stop at nothing to rid her world of four people who could put her own life in danger. Wendy had only one other trick on her side, which she was reluctant to use, and would do so only if the situation meant that she had been out-manoeuvred by the wicked old witch.

Gerald jumped up from his desk, realising that an arrival from the future was about to appear. As the mist cleared, his oldest friend, Wendy emerged into the clear air, her twenty-first century clothing changed to match the long plain dresses of 1192 AD. Wendy moved to the ornate mirror, amused at the new fashion looking back at her.

"Gerald, no time to waste. Where's the old witch? There's much to do; here's the plan." Wendy hugged her old friend, conscious of the dangers hiding within the castle.

"A plan, eh?" Gayla appeared from nowhere, moving slowly into the classroom, a smirk distorting her ugly wrinkled face. "Another into my trap. One more death will please the Queen. I'm getting a taste for unwanted bodies. I think your two heads will look perfectly matched on spikes over the ramparts. You can look down and see where King Bresdon tripped and fell to his timely death." The old witch's body started to shake as she coughed out a wheezy laugh, remembering, as daylight broke, assisting King Bresdon to an untimely death.

"So at last we meet," Wendy turned away from the old crone, making a sign with her hands as opening a book. Gerald looked on at Wendy's charade; initially his face was puzzled, before he twigged her mimed plan.

"Don't turn your back on me, time traveller, you must face what is about to happen." In a wild dramatic gesture, Gayla tossed aside her long grubby cloak, exposing the body of a growling werewolf. Its fangs were glinting as it reared on its hind legs, preparing to pounce on the defenceless duo.

"Hold my hand, Gerald, this should be fun." In her human form, Wendy uttered her final words in Gerald's classroom, as she morphed into her alter ego, Astrid. Instantly, Astrid's pages opened, sucking Gerald back into the left hand page of Time Travel, from where, many years earlier, he'd arrived.

Savouring the moment, Astrid hovered a short distance from the snarling werewolf, ready to evaporate into another place in time. Her plan was to disappear in front of the monster's puzzled gaze. Suspended in a time continuum, Wendy and Gerald watched on as Gayla's werewolf snarled at the aging old tome, suspended a few feet from her. Inside the time capsule, the fear of the death sentence Gayla had imposed on them had vanished. If they could prod a stick at the raging beast, it would complete their victory. If they were safe, their only sadness was that Gayla would return to her human form and continue to wreak danger and fear amongst the innocent folk of Palogonia.

With lightning reflexes, the werewolf leapt at the hovering old tome, snapping its jaws tightly onto its fading leather cover. As Astrid vaporised across the time continuum, its journey had three passengers: who were riding through time in relative safety, with another unwanted traveller clinging desperately on, its jaws clamped like a vice to Astrid's faded leather covers.

CHAPTER TWENTY-EIGHT

Let battle commence
2016 AD

Leaving Axle and Imogena alone, now Wendy had gone to rescue Gerald, was not going to be an issue. Billy had been briefed by Wendy and Astrid that, on his return from his time travels, he would only have missed a few seconds of current real time. Based on these facts, there was no point in disturbing the royal twins. In fact, Billy doubted whether they were aware of his presence. Axle, Imogena and Martha still sat spellbound as they watched *Madagascar: Escape 2 Africa* as a team of *military penguins* crashed their battered escape aircraft back into the African bush, laden with *Marty and his friends*.

"It's time, Martha." Billy guided Martha away from the movie to his room, eager to move ahead with the second part of his plan. Having spent several hours fine-tuning his latest App, *Time Crusaders*, Billy was convinced that he could use the latest version to overcome any dangers which the two mercenaries could throw at them. But first he must bring Martha along with him, through the time continuum, into the guts of the new App;

but only if needed. Then it would be time to test his new App, along with his time-travelling abilities. But the key ingredient must be how he could trap the mercenaries within the new game.

1192 AD

Arriving back amongst the clump of palm trees, from which they had escaped on their last attempt, Billy guided Martha to a spot where the mercenaries could be watched. This time, they would have surprise on their side, with reinforcements arriving from another source. But for Billy's plan to rescue Gandolf and Jasper to work, everyone must follow the actions agreed to the letter. There was no time for heroics or emotion; Billy had explained that this rescue must be treated like a military action.

A short distance from the tumbledown shed which the mercenaries had used as their base camp, the fishing boat Billy had used remained stuck in the sand, washed by the incoming waves. It was clear from the actions of the mercenaries that they had decided to use the deserted fishing boat to deliver their valued prisoners to Sheik Amir. Several bags had already been taken from the camels and loaded into the fishing boat. Aware that both camels were becoming increasingly agitated, the mercenaries pulled them into a clump of nearby palm trees, where they were now, even more securely tethered. As the camels struggled against the leather straps, denying their escape away from the lengthy captivity, Gandolf and Jasper screamed with pain as they were dragged against the angry beasts.

Martha watched on, with tears streaming down her freckled cheeks, as her brother yelled out for help. His sunburned body was suspended from the strapping holding him and the remaining packages. Billy pulled Martha back, as she began to exit their cover to help her long lost brother.

"Martha, that won't help, we need surprise, then we'll get them both away to safety," Billy held his hand over Martha's mouth, holding tightly around her waist with his other hand. "You must be quiet; my friends will be here soon. Just be patient, Martha."

Whatever was being stored in the remaining packages, still piled on the camels, the mercenaries considered them to be equally important as Gandolf and Jasper; they left their prisoners to be loaded last of all onto the waiting fishing boat. As the remaining packages were removed from the camels, Osbert ensured that the extra bindings taken from packages were bound around their prisoners, creating even more blood-curdling yelps of pain.

"Shut up yuh children, yuh sound like girls." Edgar placed a kick into Gandolf's ribs, laughing at the increased agony he'd delivered. "Yuh'll soon be with our friend the Sheik, then yuh can scream as 'e takes yuh apart, one limb at a time."

"Look, who are they?" Osbert pointed at two white-clothed strangers sitting cross legged along the beach, way past their ramshackle hut. "What yuh doing? Who are yuh?" Osbert screamed out, as he began making his way towards the two strangers. As he moved along the beach, the two intruders just stared out to sea, disregarding the approaching mercenary.

"Leave them, soldier, they're after your prisoners," Gayla screamed out, as she approached from another clump of palm trees. "I'm yer friend, don't go near them. You need me to fight? I've got the magic to beat them," Gayla stumbled towards the mercenaries, both now waving cutlasses, ready to destroy the new intruders.

"Come on, Martha, now's our time!" Billy dragged Martha through the cover of the remaining palm trees, towards the two shackled camels which were still retaining Gandolf and Jasper.

As Billy reached the first camel, it was frightened by Billy's approach, and began bellowing, its ear-pounding snorting attracting the attention of Edgar and Osbert, who had already been heading away from the camels, to confront their new intruders. If only Astrid's rules had allowed transporting inanimate objects through time, Billy would have brought a knife to cut through the leather bindings. During the time when Gandolf and Jasper had been tied on to the camel's packaging, the leather bindings had tightened so much that they were now impossible to untie. Nervously, Billy approached the camels as they angrily attempted to break away from the straps tethering them to the palm trees. As much as the raging camels and the pain racked prisoners tried, it was now patently clear that the bindings would never snap; a knife was the only way to release the prisoners.

Along the beach, Wendy and Gerald watched as the two mercenaries closed in on Gayla. Understanding that she was facing two determined men who were armed and prepared to kill if required, Gayla dropped to her knees, bowing in supplication to the approaching mercenaries. Watching from a short distance away, now was the time for Wendy and Gerald to move forward, creating even more confusion for Osbert and Edgar.

"Stay here, Martha, I'll be back. Trust me, I know how to finish this," Billy rubbed his thumbnails together, preparing his travel home to 2016 AD.

CHAPTER TWENTY-NINE

Time warriors to the rescue... again?
2016 AD and 1192 AD

Ripples of childish giggling echoed through to Billy's room, as Axle and Imogena absorbed even more of *Marty's* adventures. Neither had been aware of Martha's absence; they were completely locked into their entrancing new technology world. They had already fallen headlong into a world controlled by a small box with coloured buttons. Now was not the time to explore what the royal twins had gleaned from their new experiences. Billy had to prove that *Time Crusaders* worked and would achieve everything which burning the midnight oil had, hopefully, achieved.

Wendy and Gerald's mission had obviously been compromised. They had arrived in exactly the right place, a short distance away from the ramshackle hut. But just before he'd left Martha, he was sure that a third party whom he'd seen scampering into the palm trees was his nemesis, Gayla. But how? Neither his mother nor Gerald would want the evil old crone anywhere near the rescue operation. But somehow the crafty old witch had made it to the Holy Lands, slap bang into the middle of his planned rescue.

Flickering blue lights reflected around Billy's bedroom as his screens came to life. After a few calculations and several lines of programming, three screens began receiving various images from 1192 AD. Billy's Apple iMac was already displaying the home page of *Time Crusaders,* awaiting the first player to enter. Two more TV screens began delivering scenes from the Mediterranean beach, back in the Holy Lands. The largest screen showed a wide angle shot showing the two mercenaries, their cutlasses aloft standing above Gayla, the old crone, kneeling in the boiling sand, restrained by Osbert's foot. Behind the central image, back in the distance, Wendy and Gerald watched on, waiting to proceed with the next stage of Billy's plan. A smaller screen focussed on the two camels, still struggling to extricate themselves from the leather bindings, with Gandolf and Martha's brother Jasper still retained by even more leather strapping.

As part of the new App, *Time Crusaders*, Billy's Apple iMac displayed a white sanded beach with a number of pirate ships in full sail heading towards the shore, laden with heavily armed pirates waiting to attack, as yet an enemy unseen by any other party joining the game. Now for the tricky part, requiring a touch of Billy's technical wizardry. All the pirate ship's complement of brigands needed was a target, if they were to win bonus points. On the large real-time screen Billy marked the moving image showing the mercenaries and Gayla. Without hesitation, he dragged the figures across into his Apple iMac. Now part of *Time Crusaders,* already scurrying along the beach, Edgar and Osbert looked out at the approaching pirates. Between them they had one cutlass; the other had dropped as they made the transition from real time to Billy's App. But where was Gayla? Somehow she'd evaded capture by the electronic world in which Billy had entrapped the mercenaries.

Back on the main screen, where Gayla had been under attack from the two mercenaries, a massive werewolf scratched amongst the sand. The gruesome beast marked its presence, whilst pointing towards the clump of palm trees edging the beach. From the cover of the palm trees, imminent danger for the giant werewolf emerged into the picture on Billy's live screen. At least a dozen wolves, together with two Pitbull Terriers and a German Shepherd, cautiously eased themselves from their tree-lined cover. Slowly edging towards the werewolf, now standing on its hind legs, ready for any impending conflict. Billy watched on, as Gayla's alter ego bounded headlong, amongst the pack of attackers. As the snarling and squeals of agony from the bloody scrap rebounded around Billy's room, the fight disappeared past the palm trees away into the adjoining sand dunes, and then off the real-time transmission.

Realising that Gayla's alter ego had left the beach, Wendy hurried towards the spot where Gayla had metamorphosed, to locate the cutlass dropped by one of the mercenaries. Gerald struggled along the burning white sand, in an attempt to keep pace with Wendy, who was already heading towards Martha, Gandolf and Jasper, still bound to the increasingly angry 'ships of the desert'.

Edgar and Osbert looked out to sea, understanding that their task within *Time Crusaders* was, firstly, to escape the incoming conflict. If successful, they could use long spiked poles to poke holes in the incoming pirate ships, gaining extra lives for everyone they sank. Three ships approached close to the shore, almost ready to offload heavily armed pirates, intent on destroying anyone on the beach. Osbert rushed to grab the first spiked pole, ready to swim to the warship and sink it, gaining more lives. Edgar decided to attack the nearby warship, immediately swimming at great speed, spike in hand.

Within the rules of *Time Crusaders*, Billy had forgotten to warn either the mercenaries or the invading pirates that the Mediterranean was overrun with Great White Sharks.

CHAPTER THIRTY

Time to leave
2016 AD

Five triangular black and white fins swept across the screen, two submerging as they approached Osbert and Edgar. Their game over, zero points were registered for their first part of Billy's new App. As the pirate ships closed in on the shore line, the remaining Great White Sharks leapt from the water, crashing down across the decks of several of the approaching ships. Dozens of the crew jumped from the crushed vessels into the water, only to be swallowed up by the giant sharks. Along the bottom of the screen, increasing bonus points were registered for the Great White defenders of the seas. All other combatants were missing from the screen, registering zero points.

Watching the action on his Apple iMac, Billy was now satisfied that his latest App had been an overwhelming success, and confident that he could now return to the Mediterranean, and free the two prisoners. Gayla was somewhere in the Holy Land, way away from the beach. Probably she was still involved in a monumental scrap with a hungry pack of wolves and three dogs, imported from their morning exercise alongside the Mersey. Whatever magic the old crone could bring to the scrap, Billy was convinced that tackling the starving pack would take precedence with Gayla, for the time being.

Osbert and Edgar were a different matter. Moved into Billy's latest game, they had succumbed to the overpowering odds stacked against them. They were no longer a threat to Gandolf and Jasper, Billy's game providing bonus points for the Great White Sharks to emerge as winners, for the first game.

Madagascar had only moved on a few frames when Billy looked in again on Axle and Imogena. For now he must leave them alone, to allow him to catch up with his mother, Gerald and Martha. Billy smiled as he watched the two newcomers to the twenty-first century, who must soon be returned to their own time. These were resilient children, who needed the guidance of their parents to lift the spell swamping Palogonia, still feeding the needs of their evil grandmother. For Astrid had studied Palogonian history, which, it appeared, had been distorted by the magic introduced by Gayla.

1192 AD

Whizzing back through the time portal, Billy bumped onto the warm sand alongside the ramshackle hut recently deserted by the mercenaries. Along the beach, his mother, Martha and Gerald were facing stern resistance from both camels, as they attempted to cut the bindings still holding Gandolf and Jasper. As Billy approached, he watched as, once again the cutlass was knocked from his mother's hand, spinning it away into the perfect white sand.

"Stop! Wendy, get away from them, you're causing more pain to those guys." Billy struggled through the yielding sand, to join the helpless gang, watching as each movement from the camels brought even more screams of pain.

"Please, sir, you must wait for the camels to calm down, otherwise they'll kill us," Gandolf, racked with pain, struggled with the words, writhing under the movement of the irritated beast. "Whatever you do, don't cut the camels free, or they'll drag us away into the desert."

"I'll be back. Just keep back from the camels. I know how to deal with this." Billy rubbed his thumbnails, and disappeared into a cloud of white mist.

2016 AD

Lifting both angry snorting camels into *Time Crusaders* was not an issue. Billy had already developed the time portal program when he removed Osbert and Edgar from 1192 AD, bringing them across to be combatants within the App. But with great urgency, he must now find a reason for making them part of the game. Camels were beasts of burden, and were prized by Bedouins to work tirelessly as 'ships of the desert'. The answer was simple. A tribe of Bedouins would attempt to capture and tame the unmanageable beasts. Capturing the cavorting beasts, without dragging along Gandolf and Jasper, was an unwanted complication. But Billy was convinced that a few extra lines of programming would solve the problem.

As he watched, on the big screen in real time, the agony suffered by Gandolf and Jasper, his fingers dashed across the keyboard, writing two extra features for the App. On the screen, a restless tribe of Bedouins, leading four dromedary camels appeared along the water's edge. On the main screen showing real time in 1192 AD, Billy highlighted the two camels, still tethered securely to the palm trees, and, in turn, to Gandolf and Jasper. With the image of the camels held, Billy rattled out several more lines of programme, removing Gandolf and Jasper from the captured frame. On the Apple iMac two camels arrived, with leather straps dangling from the saddles, now dragging along behind. With the target of the two camels in sight, two of the Bedouins ran towards the two new arrivals, lassos in hand. Along the top of the screen, several electronic hazards, a selection of swords, and a raging sand storm dropped between the Bedouins and the two camels. Two of the pirate ships that had escaped the attack from the Great White Sharks closed towards the shore. Dozens of sword-waving brigands leapt ashore, chasing extra points for every kill. Billy smiled as *Time Crusaders* removed yet another hazard from his real-time exploits.

1192 AD

Billy's removal of the crazed camels from the Beirut beach into *Time Crusaders* required a little subtlety. Just prior to the camels' disappearing, Billy created a massive sand storm, causing everyone to lie flat in the sand, using anything to protect exposed eyes, mouths and ears. But this was no ordinary sand storm. As the boiling dust settled, Gandolf and Jasper lay alone, covered by mountains of swirling sand; neither camel was anywhere to be seen. If the two prisoners wished to believe that the camels had escaped in the storm, that would be one less explanation for Billy and his friends to deal with. With the dangers from the mercenaries removed, together with Gayla, and, now, the feral actions of the two camels a distant problem, Billy suddenly felt that all was at last going to plan.

As the dust settled, Wendy and Martha found several leather bags containing the mercenaries' water supply. Immediately they began cleaning the deep cuts caused by the leather bindings having chafed into Gandolf and Jaspers' sunburned limbs. With visibility having slowly returned, Gerald wandered into the nearby clump of palm trees, in search of other ways to treat their wounds. In no time Gerald returned to the beach, carrying a number of rotting coconuts; convinced that the decaying fruit, in the form of a creamy mess, would ease the pain from their seeping wounds.

"Listen, guys," Billy sat down in the shade of the palm trees, alongside the two rescued Crusaders. "What I'm going to tell you sounds crazy, and I don't expect you to understand, or, indeed, believe me, but we're taking you home to Palogonia."

As Wendy and Martha tended to the wounds of Gandolf and Jasper – spreading the rotted coconut juice – Billy began delivering his plan to rid Palogonia of Queen Ventenil. Occasionally, Gerald intervened when he sensed that Billy's explanation was lost on the two wounded Crusaders. To help their understanding of events back in Palogonia, Gerald carefully detailed a list of recent horrors that the Queen's regime had thrust upon the country. But the most difficult news for Gandolf was to accept the improbable news of the drugged imprisonment of his wife, Princess Xena. Gerald could sense the confusion that both Gandolf and Jasper were suffering. Having spent years in the deserts and the mountainous regions of the Holy Lands, dealing everyday with dangers from mercenaries and patrolling enemy rebels, Billy's explanation was welcome, yet difficult to accept.

But even more impossible for them to accept was the arrival of foreigners out of nowhere, freeing them from the bloodthirsty mercenaries. Gerald fully expected that trusting any crazy ideas from a bunch of strangers would be sneered at. Even Martha was still trying to come to terms with the speed and incredible sequence of the events in which she was involved. Satisfied that Martha should be left to patch up the wounds covering their arms and legs with the putrid coconuts, Wendy pulled Billy away into the palm trees, out of the earshot of Gandolf, Jasper and Martha.

"Enough talk, Billy, they're never going to believe you. Think about it, turn it on its head, how would you deal with it?" Wendy quietly insisted to her son. "We can take them back to Gerald's quarters. Then we can plan how to deal with the Queen. Oh, by the way, did you spot the necklace Gandolf's wearing? There's a silver ring attached to it."

CHAPTER THIRTY-ONE

Where's the witch?
1192 AD and 2016 AD

Queen Ventenil crashed through the heavy oak door into Gerald's quarters, followed closely by four palace guards. The only visible movement within the room came from the heavy golden window drapes swaying with the incoming breeze. Two of the guards swept past the Queen, pushing open the door into Gerald's classroom, while the other guards hurried to search his bedroom. From their expressions, it was immediately evident that Gerald's quarters were completely empty. Not a soul was to be found. There was no sign of life. Not a glass or plate, not even a slice of half-eaten bread. Nothing.

"Find the witch, NOW!" Queen Ventenil screamed out, shoving the guards from her path, as she rushed from Gerald's quarters.

2016 AD

Billy watched on the large screen from the safety of his bedroom, as Queen Ventenil stormed around Gerald's rooms, disbelieving her guards' assertions that the twin's tutor was missing. Billy's return to 2016 AD, to check out the safe return of everyone, had proved worth the effort. Now that the Queen had targeted Gerald as being involved with the disappearance of her grandchildren, it was impossible to travel back to Gerald's quarters. Even without the dangerous old witch on the horizon, Billy's initial plan would need to be thought through again.

With no means of communicating directly with Wendy and the gang waiting for him back on the Mediterranean beach, he must return and explain the problem. The more he considered the next stage, the more he was certain that transferring everyone back to 2016 AD was the answer, whilst awaiting the time to strike. But there was a major complication – Gerald. For Gerald was on a one way ticket; he could never return to the future.

CHAPTER THIRTY-TWO

Behind you, Billy!
1192 AD
The Holy Land

There was no way to hide the stark immovable facts, as Billy explained Queen Ventenil's search of Gerald's quarters, which he'd watched from the safety of the twenty-first century. Moving everyone back to the twenty-first century was just not going to happen. There was no way, having now watched the crazed antics from Queen Ventenil, that Gerald could travel alone to Palogonia. Billy's latest plan, which so far had worked, had always been to move the group as a unit back to the castle. But now the Queen had posted heavily armed guards inside and outside Gerald's quarters, making this option untenable. With daylight almost swamped by the onset of the Mediterranean night time, Billy sat on the edge of the palm trees, away from the expectant group. An eerie silence was only broken by the constant crashing of the Mediterranean along the deserted shoreline. Several times Billy had disappeared, returning with further news, each time improving the chances of the rescue mission's succeeding.

Now was not the time to convince Gandolf and Jasper of the magical possibilities which Billy and his friends had at their fingertips. Billy and Gerald had already promised to transport them back to Palogonia, where the true facts of Queen Ventenil's evil control could be seen for themselves. If it came to a physical fight, neither Gandolf or Jasper were in good enough physical shape to tackle the highly trained guards who were now surrounding the Queen. Guile, coupled with speed and the use of their time-travelling magic, must be the way to topple the Queen. But first a safe targeted landing site must be agreed.

"I've an idea, Billy." Martha moved behind Billy, both staring out into the darkness covering the crashing waves. "It's simple, Billy. You can take us to my mother's house? No one will suspect our arriving there; you know, Billy, lots of friends will help. What do you think?"

Billy continued staring into the bleakness of the Mediterranean night. For a while Martha was uncertain whether he'd listened to her idea. Slowly he turned to face Martha, grabbing her hands, his face suddenly alight with realisation that Martha had scored a bull's eye.

"Brilliant, just brilliant. Come, let's tell the others," Billy tugged Martha back into the palm trees, where the others were resting, excited at the new plan that had come from the most unexpected source.

Of course this would require a revision to the original plan. But frequently a change of direction on the battlefield will surprise the enemy, shortening the war for the winning side. Billy had no idea what to expect when they arrived in the village, dominated by the fortified castle. With the dangers which Queen Ventenil had observed with the disappearance of Gayla and Gerald, and her grandchildren apparently in some far-off land, possibly under some magic spell in the future, her defences would be on high alert. Queen Ventenil had a reputation for trusting no one. Even her favoured witch, and, sometimes sounding-board, Gayla, was only allowed knowledge on a need-to-know basis. But whatever devious plan Billy and his team conjured up, even without Gayla's magic, locating Princess Xena, with the Queen's guard on high alert, was going to be a fearsome task. But maybe Billy had another idea which could overcome the daunting possibilities ahead of them.

Billy and Martha hustled back to the group, still resting amongst the cover of palm trees. Concern, that had engulfed the group like a black shadow, immediately lifted as Billy explained Martha's idea. Already, Martha had experience travelling through time, even though she had found what she had seen back in Liverpool to be a dream. But at this stage, she was prepared to accept the journey back to her family cottage, as worth the risk. Since Gandolf and Jasper had been released from the horrors of being entrapped on the stinking camels, Martha had endeavoured to convince them of Billy's, Gerald's and Wendy's honest intentions. For what did Gandolf and Jasper have as an alternative? Just a few days ago, they had been misplaced Crusaders, left to survive alone within the constant dangers of the Holy Land. Having been rescued by what appeared to be magical powers, trusting in these strangers was the only way forward.

Martha had explained to Billy the geography of the village, and the defences they must contend with. Once back in Palogonia, Martha's home would be their base camp, while waiting for Gandolf and Jasper to regain their strength for the conflict that would lie ahead. Even with the shortage of food supplies inflicted on those living outside the castle, Martha's mother would relish rebuilding the strength of the two returning Crusaders from her hidden stashes.

Timing the return to Palogonia would be vital, as they plummeted through time, back to join village life. If the landing site was to be inside Martha's house, the consensus was that it was best to arrive during the night, while Martha's mother was sleeping. Martha could then wake her mother and gently break the news to her of the return of her son and four other guests.

There was no need to delay the journey through Astrid's time continuum. All that was required was for Billy and Wendy to locate the time and place inside the village, form a circle holding on to each other, rub their thumbs and whoosh, whizz through the time portal all together.

Two beady eyes watched on as the group formed a circle grabbing tightly to each other's clothing, for the short time journey ahead. Dragging behind Gandolf and Jasper as they began their journey, lengthy straggling leather bindings were still attached, flapping from their waists. Just sufficient for another passenger to hold on to, urgently needing to make her journey back to Palogonia.

CHAPTER THIRTY-THREE

Now you see me
1192 AD
The Kingdom of Palogonia

Like clockwork, almost to the day, the annual winter snows piled up across Palogonia. Hundreds of villagers had already been rounded up for the yearly snow clearing, from the two roads leading up to the castle. This year, as the labourers slaved away, shovelling and pushing tons of snow from the two roads, dozens of castle guards watched for possible strangers who might wish to break into the castle.

Already where the road disappeared into the village, the snow clearers had made substantial heaps of snow, as they worked away from the village, towards the castle. As the workers left behind growing piles of snow, the village children screamed with delight as they climbed the snow mountains, rolling around with shrieks of laughter. Even the castle guards, intent to extract the maximum efforts from the villagers' snow-moving labours, watched on with amusement as the children enjoyed the annual snow festival.

"Move out of my way. Don't you know who I am?" Gayla shook the snow from her clothing, arriving from her time travel, onto the peak of one of the larger snow piles, before rolling onto the slushy road. As she struggled to her feet, she disentangled a leather strap which she'd pulled from Jasper as he disappeared through the time portal ahead of her.

"I know you, yuh're the Queen's witch. She's lookin' fer you. Difficult to get to the castle yet." One of the castle guards moved sufficient distance from the bedraggled old witch.

"Leave me, just tell Her Majesty that I'm safe and I have news, only for her ears. NOW GO OR I'LL TURN YOU INTO A DOG!"

But there was no way Gayla was going to let the yearly snowfall hinder her progress. She knew that Queen Ventenil had a one-minute fuse, and, already, she might be on the Queen's kill list. There was little point attempting to explain time travel, Prince Gandolf and a young peasant boy's having escaped from the Holy Land. Then there was Billy, Gerald and the Chinese woman, all with the ability to slide through space. But she had picked up on Gerald's Achilles' heel; he couldn't return to the future. Gayla stood peering up to the castle, her clothes dripping from the melting snow. As she considered her future at the hands of the Queen's anger, she began to shiver. Warmth: that was what she needed. Of course, she had her smoke spell which she'd used once before, turning herself into a thin cloud of white smoke. That was it, she would slither her way to the castle, as a cloud of white smoke. No one would suspect her transformed shape making its way across the fresh snow fall.

CHAPTER THIRTY-FOUR

Time to think Billy
1192 AD
The Kingdom of Palogonia

Billy and Wendy left Martha and Jasper's emotional homecoming and wandered into the snow-smothered village. As they rounded one of the larger buildings, the castle came into view. In the breaking light hundreds of men, women and some children were labouring under duress from the guards, as they cleared the roads of the huge deluge of snow. One thing was certain, entry to the castle, even without the hills of snow, was a definite no go. Of course they could arrive through the time portal, but even then there would be a cast iron certainty of a pitched battle. Billy and his time friends were without weapons, and were certainly not trained as soldiers. Neither had they set out to engage in physical violence.

Gandolf appeared behind them, hobbling towards Billy and his mother; the Crusader was still weak from his years surviving in the most hostile conditions.

"Martha tells me that you have special magic from your time Billy. I don't understand, but she tells me it's a magic box and that you can make people disappear into it. She tells me that that's how the mercenaries and those stinking camels disappeared."

"Yeah, you're right. No point in trying to explain, but I think my magic is the only way we can finish what we've started." Billy offered an arm to the faltering Prince, clearly embarrassed by his physical weakness.

"Gandolf, you need a few days to build up your strength; when you're ready for a fight, Billy will be back. Oh, and your children are safe with us," Wendy eased her hand under Gandolf's elbow, offering further support on his other side.

Even with the morning sun breaking across the Eastern sky, the snowfall had lowered the temperature well below freezing. Billy remembered a snow storm that had once blocked the roads across much of Liverpool. But once the snow-clearing machines had been let loose, transport had soon been back to normal. But here in Palogonia, in 1192 AD, snow clearance took on a different meaning. Also, the villagers flimsy housing was never going to offer much shelter from the freezing temperatures.

Not only was shelter from the inclement weather vital to the group's future, but it was essential to keep hidden from the castle guards. If spotted, their fate was a cast-iron certainty. There would be no mercy, only a selection of possible ways to die. This was not a country where any due process of law existed. This was law by the rules of an evil dictator, determined to retain control by whatever means were at her disposal.

Billy's group collected around the open fire in Martha's house, which also housed a large blackened cooking pot, suspended over the blazing wooden logs. Priority was given for

Gandolf and Jasper to stay close to the flames, aiding their recovery from years of starvation and weakened bodies.

"I shall be back soon," Billy offered, knowing that there was a growing understanding that his 'magic' probably held the best chance to complete their task, ridding the kingdom of the Queen's authoritarian rule. "Gandolf, you understand that we have to rid the kingdom of your mother-in-law. Right now I don't know how, but..." Gandolf held up his hand to stop Billy.

"A woman that can lock away my wife and brainwash my children does not deserve to live. Maybe that's not how you approach things in your time, Billy, but here the only sentence must be death." Gandolf tried to ease himself from the chair positioned next to the fire, then collapsed back from overpowering exhaustion, overcome with emotion. "I trust you, Billy, I await your command."

CHAPTER THIRTY-FIVE

You'll never win time traveller
1192 AD
The Kingdom of Palogonia

Across the stone cold floors of the corridor leading into the East Wing, a trail of faint white smoke moved slowly towards a small arched oak door. Three iron bars, secured by six rusting locks, held the door firmly closed. A small cat flap was the only access into room. Using the same method of passing into secured rooms, Gayla's smoke trail slithered through the cat flap, arriving in the darkly lit room housing Princess Xena. As Gayla transformed back into her human form, the shutters covering several windows opened, pitching sunlight into Princess Xena's 'prison'. As the room filled with the morning sunlight, Gayla approached the still figure of the imprisoned Princess, who was sitting motionless next to a decorated stone fireplace, where a mound of pine logs was smouldering lifelessly away.

"Fear not, my dear, you're safe here." Gayla sidled up to the sleeping Princess, stroking her long black hair, which was shining under the sunlight beaming into the room. "Soon all will be finished. Your useless husband is marooned down in the village, and your children will be brought to me soon. Then I will be the most powerful person in the land. Even your mother cannot stop me changing history." Gayla shuffled around the chair holding the comatose Princess, laughing at the situation which she now controlled.

Gayla sat opposite Xena, glowing with the victory which she now considered hers for the taking. Xena was the obvious target for the time travellers. Several years ago, she'd warned the Queen, that if Prince Gandolf's wedding ring was placed back in Xena's left hand, in a flash the Queen would dissolve into a pile of dust. Xena would wake and become Queen of Palogonia. In fact, the ring touching Princess Imogena's left hand palm was the trigger to release the spell, but not exactly as Gayla suggested.

As she quietly pondered all the facts, it was clear that everything had played into her hands. She could play a waiting game. When the time travellers came for Xena, she would transform from the faint white smoke cloud into her favourite manifestation, Shamsac, her pet werewolf. Who could blame her for the slaughter of four royal Princes, by a hideous werewolf, last seen running into the forest along the Palo river? But the werewolf had one further target before its escape – Queen Ventenil. Nothing could then stop her from becoming Queen. Indeed, Queen Gayla would retain Prince Gandolf's ring, ensuring that she would finish off the royal house of Palogonia.

CHAPTER THIRTY-SIX

A masterpiece or nothing
2016 AD
Liverpool

Knowing that his mother, Gerald, and the two Crusaders were relatively safe, hiding in Martha's house, Billy could concentrate on his next plan. Whatever the Queen and her security could throw at them, Billy was relieved that any threat from Gayla no longer existed. Whether she was scooting around the deserts of the Holy Land, posing as a werewolf, or using her spells to anger anyone who crossed her path, she was no longer a danger to him. Whatever she was doing, the old crone was never going to be missed. When Astrid had introduced Billy to time travel, he had seen this as an adventure, not a life threatening operation. For there was no doubt that life held little value to Gayla. From his understanding of life in the Middle Ages, coupled with his real life experiences during this adventure, life was certainly cheap to those in power. Queen Ventenil had no compunction about removing any unwanted souls, if they stood in her way.

So here was the conundrum facing Billy, who was bound by the laws and morals of his twenty-first century life. Of course Queen Ventenil was undeniably an evil ruler. Billy was certain that her husband, the ever-popular and honourable King Bresdon, had not died as the result of an early morning accident, slipping from the castle ramparts. His death had Gayla's fingerprints all over the 'accident', which had immediately plunged Palogonia into a period of gloom and unrest, right across the kingdom. If only Astrid would lift the restrictions placed on his time travel, he could change the course of history in a heartbeat. But, of course, Astrid was right. Imagine modern weaponry sent to tackle medieval soldiers, armed only with swords and cross bows. The repercussions of altering the course of history would be dramatic, and would never allow for man to develop through the ages unhindered.

Billy sat in his room, pondering how Astrid's plan could succeed and yet leave history as it was documented. In all the great tomes written to record history, facts were facts, much proven by scribes who witnessed events as they occurred. Of course, some records were written with a little bias, but historical facts were in the past, and so they should stay. Of course, Billy knew that his twenty-first century hi-tech expertise could outflank most things he would face during any conflict in Palogonia. But was this right? The more he considered the task ahead, the more Billy questioned the morality of what was being proposed.

He must challenge Astrid before he took the next step and developed a piece of modern technology that would forever change the face of history. If only he could move a cell phone through the time portal, he could question Astrid without making yet another journey.

But first he must check on the twins. Again, Billy had only been away from the twins for just a few seconds in his time. There they were still enthralled, as attempts were made for *Marty and his friends* to understand where they'd now arrived in Africa. Another factor was playing on Billy's mind. Both the twins and Martha had been exposed to travelling into the twenty-first century from their time, for over four days now. Three days were left for Billy either to return them to Palogonia or to watch them dissolve into time dust.

1192 AD

As Billy crashed back into Martha's house, nothing had changed since he had whizzed home to conceive his next plan. Even though the sun was shining brightly in the eastern sky, its rays did little to melt the snow drifts surrounding the village. Martha's peasant's cottage was still feeling the effect of the above-average freezing conditions. On this arrival, the only person startled by his re-appearance was Martha's mother; the others were now used to Billy's shuttling through his time portal and arriving back without notice.

"I must speak to Astrid; we're wrong, Wendy." Billy aimed his comment directly at his mother. "We can't change the course of history; you know exactly what she said."

Wendy moved away from the fireplace, disappearing behind a threadbare sack curtain which separated the sleeping area from the remainder of the cottage. Instantly, Wendy changed form into her alter ego, Astrid the ageing leather tome, its pages open at TIME TRAVEL. As Astrid slowly hovered back through the curtains, the open pages gradually grew brighter, offering a bright yellowing glow across her pages.

"Don't be frightened, my friends," Astrid quietly offered, in her soft motherly voice. "I'm your friend; if you like, I'm your travelling magic friend." Astrid hovered towards the open fireplace, turning to face everyone, her back to the fire. "You've a problem, Billy?"

Jasper placed an arm around his mother's shaking shoulders, protecting her from the flying, talking, magic book. Everyone else kept a respectful distance, as Astrid waited to discuss Billy's concerns.

"Astrid, I have a problem. We have always agreed that wherever we travel and whatever we get involved with, we must not change written and documented history. But here we are, proposing to remove a legally appointed Queen and to replace her with her daughter, using some bizarre magic spell. I accept that bringing back Gandolf and Jasper has done nothing to alter history. But to remove a Queen? That can't be right."

Maintaining her hovering position, Astrid wobbled a little as she chuckled to herself, knowing that Billy had not fully understood the brief she set out. Or maybe she'd not fully explained the rules when offering Billy and Gerald the powers of time travel.

As Astrid continued to float just away from the fireplace, her soft delivery had already calmed the fear of the non-time-travellers. A sense of uncertainty that had initially been present in Martha's home, was turning to understanding that help might be at hand. Astrid appeared to take a breath before offering a considered response to Billy.

"Yes, my boy, those are the rules under which you and Gerald can travel through time. When we set out on this journey, you, Billy took the right hand page, permitting you to travel freely back in time and then back home. But never into the future, past your own time. And you Gerald, can only move back in time, and through the same time continuum. Agreed?"

Billy and Gerald nodded in agreement, as everyone else watched on, listening for a further explanation from the glowing pages of the old leather tome.

"There are other conditions, so as not to make historical changes. Firstly, only flesh and blood can be moved through time. The three dogs you took have had the time of their lives, Billy. This means that nothing alien to the time in history you choose, can be polluted, or offered an unfair advantage. But you're rightly questioning: why remove the Queen and reinstate the Princess? Well you need to go one step further back. Why not reinstate King Bresdon? The answer is simple, Billy; all you've seen is a dream, a mirage if you prefer, under a spell created by Gayla to take control of the Kingdom. Once you have removed the Queen by placing Gandolf's ring on Xena's palm, the spell will be broken, and history will be restored. To assuage your conscience, Billy, no one dies. Now you can achieve the victory we are seeking, by just placing the ring on Xena's hand. But the magic spell needs a little help. Billy, you need to make magic with your computer. Up to you, my son. Oh, by the way, you were all a little sloppy on your journey back with Gandolf and Jasper. Gayla latched onto a dangling leather binding on Jasper's leg and hitched a lift. She's hiding away from the Queen, and waiting for you to make your next move. Good luck, my friends."

Slowly the old tome closed, extinguishing its glowing pages. With a puff of white dust, all that was once an ageing leather tome, drifted into the orange flames of the fireplace. With Astrid's explanation to her mystified audience complete, no one noticed as Wendy silently moved back into the room, passing through the threadbare curtain.

"I'll be back, now that I know what I need to do." Again Billy evaporated, back into the future.

CHAPTER THIRTY-SEVEN

Outside the castle
1192 AD
The Kingdom of Palogonia

From inside Martha's cottage, the noise level increased, as an excited discussion ensued, following Astrid's appearance and her explanation of the facts which they were facing. Even Gerald was shocked by Astrid's disclosure that everyone living in Palogonia was in fact existing within a dream sequence created by Gayla. Even the Queen was part of the hallucination created by the evil old crone. Gandolf, Jasper, Martha and her mother had to make sense of Billy, Gerald and Wendy's ability to move through time. But now they were being asked to accept that in fact they were living within some form of fictional story.

The more the facts were debated, the more heated became the exchange of views. As everyone's differing opinions became more polarised, the louder everybody's voices resonated around the tiny cottage. With the increasing intensity of the argument, no one considered that their screaming voices were reaching across the heaped snow, besides the road leading to the castle.

It was only a matter of time, before the ruckus booming out from the tiny cottage attracted unwanted attention. As the flimsy cottage door crashed down, ten men from the Queen's heavily armed private protection unit smashed their way in. Screaming arguments, which had brought the Queen's elite troops to Martha's cottage, turned to screams of agony. One by one, the Queen's soldiers forced everyone face down onto the dirt floor; swords drawn, ready for use on anyone attempting escape.

"Don't even consider getting up; I can deliver you dead or alive, no difference to me. Now let's see what we have here," the Captain of the unit dragged Jasper's arm, turning him face up. "And who are you, skinny runt? Your name, now!"

"I'll be back, Gerald, I'll take Martha's mother," Wendy whispered softly in Gerald's ear.

"Shut up, woman, or you'll taste my sword," the Captain moved across the room towards Wendy, ready to smash his leather boot into her back. As he swung his foot towards her, to his shock he tumbled backwards as the space where Wendy and Martha's mother had been lying was now covered by a thin cloud of white mist. As the Captain thumped down onto the dirt floor, an eerie silence fell across the tiny cottage. There was a mixture of shock from Gandolf, Jasper and Martha, as her mother, led by Wendy, took flight into the future. If the captors were astonished by Wendy and Martha's mother whizzing off into the future, nine highly trained body guards edged back towards the door, their faces white with fear from the unknown black magic now facing them.

As the Captain struggled to his feet, he cautiously stood back from his prisoners, unsure whether the possibility of latent magic still hung in the air. Gerald clawed his way to a standing position, using support from Gandolf and Martha, smiling at the simple piece of time travel magic which Wendy had performed. But even with the slight advantage of shock and surprise, they were still overpowered prisoners, certain to be taken from the cottage to face more physical abuse from the Queen.

"There's more magic, Captain, but not yet. I think you should treat my friends with a little dignity, sir," Gerald eased his way towards the Captain, the senior officer now back in control, after his embarrassing mix-up with Wendy's enchanting time-traveller trick. "Captain, we'll not cause you trouble, so no more violence, please."

"I'll give the orders; now stand back, old man. I think I know who you are. You're the teacher the Queen's looking for. Your head will soon be on a pike. Now stand together, face each other. Shackle them and don't be gentle. I'll show them magic."

"Now listen, do as he says, all hold together," Gerald turned slightly smiling across at the Captain. "Was nice knowing you, Captain." Gerald started rubbing his thumbnails together. "Take me to my quarters, with a thunderous flash," were Gerald's last words uttered within the cottage.

As chanted by Gerald, the requested blinding flash and destination orders, shot the four prisoners out of the freezing cottage, away from the village, and into the relative comfort of his quarters on the west side of the castle. In the village, blinded by the brilliant white flash, ten petrified guards tumbled out of Martha's cottage, scattering in different directions to escape the possibility of yet more deathly magic. Even their senior officer scrambled on his knees, away from the cottage, into the slushy snow, his eyes stinging from the effects of Gerald's thunderous flash.

As Gerald, Gandolf, Jasper and Martha bounced into Gerald's quarters, their freedom was short lived. From behind the curtains, and scurrying out from Gerald's classroom, even more of the Queen's guard piled into the room, surrounding the new arrivals; their swords were drawn, ready for any escape attempts. Their journey, escaping from the guards in the village, had dumped them bang into a trap set by the Queen. This time, there was no possibility of a collective disappearance. For each one of them was herded to separate corners of the room, with several guards holding each one of them firmly captive. There was no escape.

"Get Her Majesty, she'll want to see who we've caught. Now!" the Captain of the guard screamed at one of his lieutenants, shoving him towards the door. "HURRY!"

Gerald slumped down onto the stone floor, his frail body slipping from the grip of two hefty guards. Across the room, Gandolf had already begun to resist the attention of two guards, his arms pinned behind him, forcing him to bend forward. Along from the main door, Jasper had already been forced to the ground, his wrist securely bound behind his back. One of the guards was pressing heavily with his leather boot between his shoulder blades, forcing the weakened young man to squeal in discomfort. Martha was pushed against the bedroom door, three guards smiling as they enjoyed the struggle put up by the beautiful young peasant girl.

"Leave my brother, you beasts, Billy's coming for you, you'll see. He'll get you, every one of you." The more Martha screamed and resisted her captors, the more pressure was applied by the three guards, each enjoying the young girl's fighting to break free.

"Listen to me," Gerald wriggled away in an attempt to loosen the grip by the hulks still pinning him to the cold stone floor. "Wendy's back with Billy and they'll be here soon. Gandolf, your children are safe. Neither Gayla nor the Queen can touch them."

"So you have returned to me!" Queen Ventenil stood defiantly in the doorway, glaring at the scene unfolding in the tutor's quarters. "And my dear son-in-law, how timely of you to return. Now do I kill you first, or your wife? Or maybe I should get in the mood with the cleaner girl and the tutor? Now let me think," smiling at her victory, she cruised elegantly around, her fingers flicking at each of her prized captives.

Only Gerald noticed the slither of faded white smoke settle just a few feet from him, spiralling itself around the leg of the guard closest to the main door.

CHAPTER THIRTY-EIGHT

Astrid's history lesson
2016 AD
Liverpool

"Have you seen this, Wendy?" Billy had opened a page from Wikipedia, relating to the history of Palogonia in the twelve century. "Well, of course, you and your alter ego knew this all the time. King Bresdon was sixty-nine when he died, and Queen Ventenil was seventy-four. Xena succeeded her father as monarch, and, furthermore, Wendy, with her husband, the Prince Regent Gandolf, they had six children. Makes nonsense of what we're dealing with, Wendy. So what'll I do?"

Billy slumped back in his chair, confused at Wikipedia's confirmation of Astrid's history lesson. "Gayla has the whole thing covered; she's indestructible, Wendy. All the other players in this game are on self-destruct, under her spell. Surely if I trap the old crone into an App, I'll think of some plot, then, surely, the rest sorts itself. All we need is for Gandolf to find his wife and pass her the wedding band. Is that it?"

Wendy moved across to Billy's bed and sat leaning against the headboard. A cloud of lightly-tinted white smoke surrounded the bed, converting his mother, once again, to a tattered leather tome, hovering just above Billy's bed. Astrid opened her pages, once again glowing in the dim light of Billy's room.

"In truth, Billy there's no easy way forward. Somehow, you've got to capture the two current dangerous parties, even if one of them doesn't know that she has an enemy. With Gayla and the Queen captured inside one of your Apps, they can do no harm. Then we can help Gandolf to go in search of his wife. But this is electronic warfare, Billy, things will change as the battles rages. Even I don't have all the answers."

"Yeah, got that. But what do I do then? Gayla's got to be locked forever in the App, and somehow the Queen must be returned to her real place in history. Is that how you see it?" Billy sat on his bed just inches away from the old leather tome who had changed the direction of his life.

"Billy, you'd better take a look at Gerald's rooms, and the cottage. Things will already have moved on," Astrid suggested in her quiet motherly tone.

As the screens around Billy's room burst into life, one began showing real time at Martha's cottage, where the Captain was all alone, scouring the empty cottage in search of his prisoners. When the second screen began transmitting real time from 1192 AD, Billy's plans were again thrown into to disarray. For not only had Gandolf, Jasper, Gerald and Martha been captured by the Queen's bodyguards, but the Queen herself was moving between her prisoners, enjoying her moment of conquest. But unseen by Queen Ventenil and her guards, a slithering white cloud had already enveloped one of the guards. Although the physical presence of the guard still remained on watch by the door, Gayla had metamorphosed into the soldier's body. Gerald watched as the unseen transformation took place; knowing that, at this stage, nothing was to be gained by exposing the old witch, for no one would ever believe him.

Wendy, now back in her human form, watched, as Billy focussed in on the fading thin layers of white smoke covering the unsuspecting guard. No explanation was required; Billy and Wendy had watched Gayla transform into one of the Queen's bodyguards. As the image closed in on the bodyguard, Gayla smiled cynically, directly into the 2016 AD 'point of view'. No longer was Queen Ventenil in charge; the game was changing rapidly. Gayla was now number one, and was moving towards her goal, total domination of Palogonia.

CHAPTER THIRTY-NINE

Another time traveller
2016 AD
Liverpool

Neither of the twins noticed the old lady sitting beside them, staring in total disbelief at the images shining back at her from the wall. Although she had understood back in her cottage that Martha's friends had the royal children safe, Martha's mother had never set eyes on either of them and could only assume that these were the Queen's grandchildren. Wendy sat beside the confused old lady, now dressed in casual clothes from the twenty-first century. There was little to discuss with the old lady, who, like the royal children was completely transfixed by *Marty and his friends*. But time was running out. Under three days and counting, with 'D-Day' looking closer and more desperate for the citizens of Palogonia.

Wendy knew that Billy needed space and solitude to work on the next App. This time, there was no second chance. There was no time for detailed research and development. But most of all, time was his biggest enemy. As he mulled over the format the new App would take, he cast an eye at the 1192 AD real-time images from Gerald's quarters and from Martha's cottage, back in the snow-covered village.

1192 AD

At the cottage, the forlorn figure of the captain of the Queen's guard stood motionless, his face twisted by the anger boiling within him. His next move would go some way to repair the humiliation which he had suffered, together with his men. With the help of several long cooking spoons and a small shovel, he forced a pile of blazing logs from the fire, pitching them around the cottage. In just a few moments, Billy's screen was blanked out by clouds of dense black smoke. A number of well-placed logs had already created an inferno, which, within minutes, would destroy the cottage that had been the Castleman family home for many years.

Back in Gerald's quarters, the Queen's new prisoners were beginning their forced journey, dragged by the guards towards the Queen's side of the castle. As the last guard made his way to the door, he turned and waved, as though knowing the position of Billy's camera. Changing the point of view of his cameras was not going to be an issue for Billy. In a short time, both screens carried incoming pictures, one of the approaching guards with their prisoners, painfully dragged. The other camera captured a point of view from behind the departing group.

2016 AD

As Billy watched the procession continue across the castle, he knew that, at this stage, there was nothing further he could do to help his friends. Now he must rush through a design for a new

App that would allow Palogonia to retain its documented history, ridding the Kingdom of the evil that radiated from every breath taken by Gayla. She had to be destroyed before the old crone allowed pointless killing to be carried out by Queen Ventenil, operating under Gayla's merciless spells. Unless matters were fixed, Gayla would be the ruler of Palogonia, and history would be re-written in the form which she had planned.

CHAPTER FORTY

Hurry Billy, the odds are piling against you
2016 AD
Liverpool

Billy paced along Brodie Avenue, a tree-lined avenue just a short distance from the family home. Even the forever-friendly scouse greetings which he encountered passed over his head, as, deep in thought he pondered the form which his new App must take. On and on he wandered, pacing the residential streets of Garston, puzzling over the way to entrap the devious old witch. Each time Billy had designed games, which now appeared in the form of Apps on his Apple iMac home page, he had only to compete against his own ideas within the games. But now he was being asked to design the most deadly accurate App, that must out-think one of the most dangerous minds he'd ever encountered. Furthermore, in truth, the competition didn't really exist. If Astrid was to be believed, his actions would return Palogonia's history to the facts he'd read about on Wikipedia. But failure would mean its history being instantly re-written. On the other hand, if he was successful in ridding the kingdom of the old witch's curses, then the Palogonian royal family would exist as shown in his recent research.

From his understanding of the recent real time images from the castle, Gayla was already several moves ahead. Although Billy, and, certainly Gerald, were fully aware of Gayla's having posed as a royal guard on escort duty with the prisoners, her next move was anyone's guess. If she could metamorphose instantly into a werewolf or one of the Queens' guards, he could only attempt at guessing what other tricks she might have up her wicked sleeve. Moreover, her smirking looks, back in the direction of Billy's 'point of view' camera, made it certain that she wanted this stage of her plan visible, for Billy to watch her every move. The old crone was enjoying the challenge, and clearly longing for a battle.

But this would change. Billy could sense that the old crone was moving her chess pieces, readying for her *coup de grace*. Gandolf appeared to hold the key to Gayla's checkmate. With him dead, and the ring still hanging from the necklace worn under his tunic destroyed, the kingdom would be hers. Removing the Queen and her grandchildren would follow. So why not allow the Queen to kill off the problem, and kill her son-in-law? Billy assumed that Gayla had considered that a Queen could not be connected to murder, particularly killing her daughter's husband. But maybe there was something, within the spell holding Princess Xena captive, that was the key to Gayla's calculated movements.

As Billy arrived back home, his mind, earlier over-laden with potential possibilities, had cleared. Now he knew the way forward. He'd field tested his Apps working in the twelfth century. He'd mastered moving real time bodies across to a live

App, both from the twelfth and twenty-first centuries. All that was now needed was the game plan, and several good guys set up in the App, ready to meet and destroy the old crone forever.

1192 AD

As the procession entered a large room forming part of the East Wing of the castle, each of the prisoners collapsed onto the freezing stone floor. Even the four remaining guards were showing signs of exhaustion, after manhandling the four prisoners across the castle, along an endless route of darkened corridors. Only one of the guards, with beady red eyes, remained standing, the others took advantage of the chance to rest against the granite walls, whilst waiting for further orders, for the next stage of the mission.

Gayla silently watched the inactivity, knowing that she must wait for her opportunity to move her plan forward. As she ambled between the four prisoners, only Gerald took notice of her latest physically reformed alter ego.

"Like the uniform, Gayla, suits you. Better than a werewolf, eh?" Gerald moved to stand up, only to be kicked back to the floor by another guard. Gayla smiled at the old tutor, saying nothing, watching the punishment dished out for breaking silence and attempting a defiant move.

"He's gone mad; guess he's seeing ghosts," the guard closest to Gerald shook his head, giving the aching tutor another firm kick in the ribs.

Gayla just smiled back at the guard, remaining silent, knowing that soon he must also die as part of her plan. But first, she must wait for the Queen to return, before commencing the first phase of the new 'Queen Gayla' ruling the Kingdom of Palogonia.

CHAPTER FORTY-ONE

I've got it!
2016 AD
Liverpool

Axle and Imogena, together with Martha's mother, stared blankly at the wall-mounted TV, as the credits from *Madagascar: Escape 2 Africa* rolled slowly up towards the ceiling. Although the twins had reached an adequate literary standard, reading many of the boring books which Gerald had introduced into their lessons, there was confusion over the scrolling words showing on their bewildered young faces. But for Martha's mother, the moving words were purely images from another world.

Billy barged into the room as the credits continued to disappear from the screen, accompanied by the remaining sound track. "Don't worry guys, there's another one, *Madagascar 3: Europe's Most Wanted;* best one of the lot I reckon."

Now must be the time to introduce the royal twins into the story of Palogonia, if the life recorded in the history books was to be believed. Even though they were indulged children, still unaware of the ways of the world, now must be the time for them to earn their birthright. The giant TV screen turned black; a quiet buzzing following the completed sound track was now the only interruption to Billy's explanation of the next stage of his plan to rid Palogonia of the wicked old crone.

"Come on, guys, let's broaden your education, follow me. And you, Martha's mum, you're part of the story." Billy eased the three refugees from Palogonia into his room, where both his large screens were already receiving hazy images from across the time continuum. One screen displayed Gandolf, Jasper, Gerald and Martha, each held captive by a heavily armed guard. On the other screen, a 'point of view' appeared to be following the Queen along a dimly lit corridor, surrounded by a collection of hangers-on and another four hefty bodyguards.

As both images eventually came into focus, Martha's mother collapsed onto her knees, praying at the sight of her two children, obviously in pain, as the guards pressed them roughly against the stone flooring. Another guard, exposing red glowing eyes, ambled between the prisoners, dishing out additional punishment, fully aware of being watched by time travellers, hundreds of years in the distance.

"The large man in the corner, held face down, is your father?" Billy placed his arms around the twins' shoulders, trusting that he could offer an element of comfort, seeing their father close up, for the first time. "Don't worry, Imo, he'll soon be free from these monsters."

Billy mulled on exactly how much of the truth he could thrust upon them. All three had experienced time travel, and had had their 'time passports stamped' from slipping through Astrid's time portal. At some stage, he must involve them, without turning them into non-believers. One thing at a time.

Wendy stared at the TV in her living room, its giant body playing a wavering black screen to an empty room. Through the door leading into Billy's hi-tech bedroom, voices could be heard, as Billy eased the nervous trio into the story that was to become part of their lives. Wendy listened carefully as her son, bit by bit, unloaded the facts that must form part of their plan to liberate Palogonia. As he continued to deliver the facts of the situation facing them, Wendy sensed that her son needed to prove the existence of his powers. A step by step approach was the way forward. Wendy knew that, once her alter ego had proven herself, Billy could start to work, explaining the way in which his Apps would be the saviour of their country.

Astrid glided quietly into Billy's room, sidling up beside him. As Astrid hovered alongside Billy, it was obvious that her appearance would cause concern. Billy smiled as his mother's alter ego rested against his right arm, the old tome wide open at TIME TRAVEL, displaying her usual glowing pages.

"Guys, you remember? This is Astrid, my good friend. She's the one who brought us in to fight the old crone, Gayla." Billy led Astrid across the room, placing her on one his desks, supported by his Apple iMac. "We need to find where the Queen has hidden your mother. You understand, Axle? You remember telling me that you were kept away from the east wing? Maybe that's where they're hiding her. Look, what Astrid is going to produce is a model of the east wing, so that I can start looking for your mother."

Astrid changed from her supported position, lying flat on Billy's desk, two glowing pages facing up. Slowly, a three dimensional model began to grow from her pages. As the model became more detailed, the walls of each room became transparent, allowing a view through several floors of the castle and dozens of rooms leading from the main corridor. Both twins' apprehension soon lifted, as the model of the east wing, growing from Astrid's pages, slowly changed direction. Dozens of rooms came into view as Astrid's model panned wider across the castle.

"Look Axle, I was just there when Gayla turned me back." Imogena prodded the model, starting back as her hand disappeared through the hologram that Astrid had created.

"Clever, eh?" Billy placed his hand on Imogena's shoulder. "Just a bit of friendly magic. Anyway, you recognise that spot? Let's start looking along that corridor, from where you were stopped. I reckon your mother's close by."

"Billy, I can see the Princess, behind that bolted door. Children, it looks like we've found your mother." Astrid, for the first time, spoke to the children in her usual calm motherly voice. "Look, there she is, sleeping and safe."

Neither of the royal children could remember their mother, for they had been just a few months old when their grandmother had taken them under her control. Already they were attempting to comprehend what they were watching, rising from Astrid's pages. Could this be a moving picture of their mother, back in Palogonia? As they prodded their hands into the hologram, in an attempt to touch their mother, their hands passed through the image of the room and their mother. Whatever the royal children were mumbling to each other, now was not the time to disturb the emotion sweeping over them. For here was their mother, the person their grandmother had repeatedly told them had died.

"Wow, now we can save your mum, guys. Astrid, that was awesome, you must show me that trick sometime." Billy excitedly moved across to his Apple iMac, now ready to design his new App and rid the Kingdom of Palogonia of the walking, talking evil that was Gayla.

CHAPTER FORTY-TWO

One hour before the knife falls
1192 AD
The Kingdom of Palogonia

"What have they told you?" Queen Ventenil swept into the room retaining her four prisoners. To a man, each of her body guards struggled to their feet, making sure that they were tightly gripping each of the securely bound prisoners.

"Nothing, you have nothing from this scum?" the Queen screamed into the face of the nearest guard, whose red eyes stared back into hers, causing the Queen to shudder under a violent spate of anger.

"You idiots, you're supposed to be my handpicked royal protection guards! Out of my way!" Her temper fully out of control, she grabbed at Martha, pulling her to her feet.

There was nothing her friends could do to stop the Queen's actions. Each of the guards gripped each of their charges even more tightly, petrified that they could be the next to feel the full force of their Queen's ruthless impatience.

"Listen to me, cleaner girl; I want my grandchildren here, now! No excuses, no lies. And I want the man they call Prince Billy," she raged on. "All your lives are expendable, cleaner girl. Do you understand?"

Martha looked across at Gerald, who was already smiling. Prince Billy! Now there's a turn up, Gerald thought to himself. Trying to stop himself from choking with laughter at the thought, Gerald began feigning a deep coughing fit, knowing full well that there was a reasonable chance that the scene was being transmitted, in real time, back to Liverpool. Gerald could only imagine Wendy's hilarious reaction to the news of Billy's "royal parentage".

"I shall give you one chance, cleaner girl. Back in the tutor's room, the old witch told me that there's a special mirror that sends pictures and people across time. You, guard, take her to the room. One hour. Listen to me, cleaner girl. If there's no Prince Billy and both my grandchildren, then I shall have Prince Gandolf's head removed and thrown to the pigs. You understand? By the way, cleaner, your darling brother will be holding the sword. Executing a royal prince? A certain death penalty, don't you think?" Queen Ventenil grabbed Martha by her long blond hair, pitching her into the arms of the guard with the red glowing eyes. "One hour!"

2016 AD

"Prince Billy, eh?" Wendy chortled. "My liege, may I have an audience?"

"That's gotta be the old crone. What story has she told the Queen? Very funny, Wendy. Amusing, eh? Seriously Wendy, I've got to move fast, now. Martha's on her way to Gerald's room with Gayla, that's for sure. One hour, she said. Axle, Imogena, no time to watch the next *Shrek* right through. This is what we're going to do. I hope you like big scary beasts, spitting bolts of flame?"

1192 AD

Still in the form of one the guards, Gayla dragged Martha across the East Wing of the castle, eventually arriving at the West Wing, and Gerald's quarters. As they passed other guards, whatever comment was thrown at them, Gayla said nothing. On a few occasions, when Martha attempted to resist, and speak to others, the red-eyed guard yanked her even more callously towards their destination.

Eventually, they made it to Gerald's unlocked rooms. Once inside, Gayla slammed the heavy oak door shut, throwing Martha into a heap against the steps leading to Gerald's school room. No longer was a red-eyed guard standing menacingly above Martha; he was now replaced by Gayla, who had instantly changed back to her real hideous form.

"My God, I should have known it was you. Werewolf, Queen's guard. What next, you evil witch?" Martha struggled to her feet, her body pained by the continual rough treatment.

"What do you want of me, witch? And who is this Prince Billy the Queen mentioned? She's as wicked as you. All she wants is Prince Gandolf's ring, the rest is a myth, probably made up by your evil mind."

"I know you can't bring the man called Billy here, my dear. It's all irrelevant. We just wait here, for more than an hour, and I shall have what I need. I've seen the ring my dear, hanging around his neck." Gayla, now in relaxed mood, dragged Martha into Gerald's bedroom, closing and then locking the door. Just sit and wait, nothing more, then let matters resolve themselves in her direction. Everything was just an hour away from 'Queen Gayla' taking the throne of Palogonia.

One of the guards would decapitate Prince Gandolf, handing the bloodied sword to Jasper, but not before Queen Ventenil had removed the ring hanging around Gandolf's neck. With the ring in her possession, her reign as Queen would be maintained. Or so she thought. Gayla had other plans for the ring, and, indeed for Queen Ventenil. Gerald and Jasper could spend their last few days watching the rats scampering around the dungeon's darkest fungal cells. As for Martha, she must die slowly and painfully. Wherever her grandchildren were, she could wait and plan how to kill them. With the ring in her possession, all bets were off for Princess Xena's children.

2016 AD

Billy found the *Shrek trailer* on line and quickly shuffled through to the rescue sequence of the imprisoned princess by *Shrek and Donkey*. Axle and Imogena watched on, initially with fear, and then with laughter, as the relationship with *Shrek, Donkey and the Dragon* developed.

"OK guys, two dragons should do the job. What do you think?" Billy looked for a reaction. Martha's mother, rapt at the *Shrek trailer*, now transferred to the main screen in Wendy's living room.

"This is my devious plan, guys. You're both going across into Gerald's rooms. I'll take you there and then disappear. Once you're there, Gayla will think all her Christmasses have come at once. But here's the clever bit. I'll lift you, and whatever form she takes, into the App. That's in here, right in my computer."

Billy could feel the excitement building up. Even the twins were showing an eagerness to get moving and to help save their parents.

"But don't worry, kids, Gayla won't harm you, as she's relying on your grandmother to carry out the dirty work. We've got time, but only about forty-five minutes, before your grandmother makes her first move. Ready? You remember the plan, once you're back in the castle? Good, let's rock 'n' roll. Oh, never mind, I'll explain when all this is over."

1192 AD

Gerald was fully aware that Billy, and probably Wendy, would be watching and listening, back in 2016 AD, in real time. But he just wished that Billy had developed portable two-way voice communications. There was so much he needed to agree with Billy, to assist with any of the plans which he knew were being formulated. Gerald watched as Gandolf sat motionless, staring directly into the face of his mother-in-law. Whatever expression he portrayed, beneath were layers of deep hatred, layered with a bursting determination to rid the country of her evil and save his wife and children.

Jasper having lived and survived in the Holy Lands along with Gandolf, a close bonding and in-depth understanding now existed between them. Jasper, although bound tightly, wriggled his position, so that he too had face-to-face contact with Queen Ventenil.

Silence prevailed. Her prisoners were awaiting any sign of a rescue attempt, which they hoped was being planned from somewhere in the future. Three guards, although cold and exhausted, were still trying their best to remain vigilant, watched over by their impatient Queen. With her nervousness building, Queen Ventenil strode silently around the freezing room, convinced that she was just a heartbeat away from removing any claim to her reign as Queen.

"Thirty minutes. Soon, my dear son-in-law, you shall be the first to fall." She moved close enough to see his fixed stare. Not a morsel of his face flinched, as she moved within inches of him.

2016 AD

Billy held the twins close to him, as he rubbed his thumbnails together, mumbling to himself. "Take me to Gerald's room, behind the long golden curtains."

"Here you go, guys, I'm with you. Be over soon, don't forget what a pincer move is. Don't wait for my instructions, just leap into action." Billy held their hands as they whizzed towards their destination, through his directional time portal.

1192 AD

Having sped through time back to 1192 AD, the twins stood behind Gerald's flapping curtains. Nothing further was uttered, as Billy shoved the twins, tumbling, into the Gerald's living room.

As instructed, they rolled dramatically over and over, landing against the legs of the old witch. Pretending surprise and shock, they huddled together, a performance that Billy now watched, back in the future, smiling with delight and pride. Stage one complete.

Hey Ho – Young Scousers to the rescue.

CHAPTER FORTY-THREE

THE FINAL BATTLE
2016 AD

Billy was now fully screened up. Three incoming screens were each displaying real time scenes from 1192 AD, ready to become the next ingredients of his latest App, *The Final Battle*. In the first, three prisoners were being watched over by Queen Ventenil and her royal protection guards. His next screen was receiving a wide angle view from Gerald's quarters. There, an over-confident Gayla was gloating at her new royal captives. But now, as part of Billy's planned battle site, a further screen burst into life. From a raised camera 'point of view', the screen was already delivering a faultless real-time view across the castle ramparts.

On his desk, already displayed on Billy's 27-inch Apple iMac, *The Final Battle* was tuned in and ready for action, awaiting the arrival of the combatants, to retain the documented history of Palogonia. A plain black computer screen gradually began to take shape, as a mirror image of the third screen from the ramparts. On either side of the Billy's screen stood two stone towers. On the right hand tower was the white flag of Palogonia, flapping against the white flagpole, proudly bearing two doves sitting within a laurel wreath. On the far left hand tower, the new black royal flag of 'Queen Gayla', displaying four scorpions, each poised to strike. Between the two towers, the main battlements were empty. The only signs of life were a number of beacons, lighting the vast area.

1192 AD

Gayla jumped to her feet, pushing away the twins, as though invaded by a herd of diseased animals. Following Billy's orders to the letter, they cowered lower, brushing the floor, in an act of total supplication. With her newly-delivered prisoners under her control, Gayla considered why the twins had been dumped into her space. So far, Billy and his team had proven more than difficult opponents. In her opinion, they were only just a match for her evil cunning and well practised magic. If this was a fortuitous mistake she'd stumbled on, now was the time to add her newly delivered victims to her plans. But how? Maybe, she should just wait until the Queen had removed Prince Gandolf from the scene. Then all was hers, to decide the fate of the remaining players in the battle for control of Palogonia.

That was it. She had Martha locked away in the old tutor's room, two children soon to beg for their lives, whilst Queen Ventenil was preparing to execute an innocent Prince. Who could touch her? All the winning cards were stacked on her side of the table. Any physical attack on her could be answered by her alter egos. She could call on at least three. There was Shamsac, her well tested werewolf, or maybe Crassky, her python, although he was yet to be fully tested in conflict. But her favourite, although she had yet to metamorphose into her new pet, was Tenatos, a fully grown tyrannosaurus.

Also well tested, now, was her ability to transform into a trail of white smoke. Whatever they threw at her, she would be ready, if a physical attack materialised from the time travellers. But why would they get involved? What benefit would they gain? Prince Gandolf was back in Palogonia, although he was soon to feel the edge of a sharp steel blade. Both the royal children were under her control, whilst the cleaner girl could become a test bed for another of her proven death spells.

"Just fifteen minutes, dear son-in-law." Queen Ventenil stroked his mud-splattered hair, expecting a reaction which she could punish. Nothing; Gandolf remained motionless, offering not a flicker of recognition.

"Not going that well, your majesty, eh?" Gerald chirped in, before receiving a kick, for speaking without permission, from his guard.

"You'll not beat us; Billy and his army will be here soon. Plenty of time," Jasper piped in, knowing that his retribution would be similar to that administered to Gandolf.

"SILENCE! Or I shall execute you all – NOW!" Queen Ventenil began shaking with uncontrollable anger, feeling that for some unfathomable reason she was losing the high ground. And what was she doing, locked in a freezing unheated ante-room, away from the comfort of her royal quarters?

"Ten minutes, and all of you will have your treacherous heads spiked, then smothered in pig's mud, suspended from the castle walls. YOU SHALL NOT DEFEAT ME!"

2016 AD

Billy sat staring into the screen of his Apple iMac, slowly nodding his head, a smile spreading from ear to ear. Without knowing it, he'd cracked the answer to beat Astrid's number one time traveller's rule. *'Only flesh and blood can travel through time'*. It was staring him right in the face, for there were no such rules within his App games. That was it, suddenly a new world of opportunities opened up: a way to outsmart Gayla. Without realising the consequences, he'd already sent pirates' galleons into battle. Cutlasses had been used by the marauding pirates. Not to forget a shoal of hungry sharks. There'd been not a word from Astrid, complaining of any broken rules. Inside a game, the characters were electronic playthings. No one actually died, they just became a series of tiny dots, inside a box of computer gizmos, some destined to a hard drive, lost amongst a myriad of unwanted bytes.

But time was now an issue. There was no doubt that Queen Ventenil would carry out her threat to rid herself of Prince Gandolf. According to the time line running along the bottom right hand corner of his Apple iMac, there were just twelve minutes left. One screen showed Gandolf, Jasper and Gerald, who were still being forcibly retained by the three guards. From her expression, it was clear that Queen Ventenil was now decidedly impatient, wanting to dispense with Gandolf. To Billy, the answer was simple. It had already been proven by his previous experience, when he had removed the camels into his App, *Time Crusaders*. At the same time, he released the bindings holding all three prisoners.

Billy focussed on the Queen's room, targeting all three guards as his first target. With a new line of programming, coupled to a rapid swipe across from the real time screen, the first elements were captured, and were now held for ever on his screen within*The Final Battle.*Looking slightly lost, three guards stood on the battlements, awaiting the next stage of the game. Now part of *The Final Battle*, all three guards made their way to the left-hand side of the screen, part of Gayla's first team of armed defenders.

1192 AD

With the guards having disappeared from right under her nose, Queen Ventenil stared at her three prisoners, standing tall and free: liberated men, their bindings gone, impending death sentences yesterday's news.

"I think you've a problem your majesty. All alone you see, your guards flown away. You'll never understand our magic." Enjoying the moment, Gerald waved his freed arms, easing the stunned Queen into the only chair in the room. "All will become clear, your majesty. But first, you will stay here, until 'Prince Billy' has woven his magic."

2016 AD

"Right, next one into the game. A damsel in distress, me thinks. What do you think, Wendy? Good plan?"

Billy was now on a roll. Already, all three guards, armed with heavy fighting swords, were patrolling under the flag designated for 'Queen Gayla'. On the second real-time screen, Martha had now joined the twins and Gayla in Gerald's living room. Martha, standing close by Gayla, with the twins still playing scared, huddled together against the stone wall.

"Perfect, here it comes guys, join the party." With another swift movement, assisted by two lines of programming, Billy's next characters appeared within *The Final Battle*.

1192 AD

Now alone, Axle and Imogena climbed from the floor, nervous and excited that the first stage had worked perfectly.

Right on cue, the old witch and Martha had disappeared in a cloud of white smoke. By now, if Billy was still in control, Martha would be held to ransom somewhere along the castle battlements, but not in a form they could comprehend, inside one of Billy's magic boxes. Billy had already explained that once he'd primed the scene, ready for their entry into the game, they'd feel a slight tingling feeling, then: whoosh, the fun could start.

2016 AD

Wendy peered over Billy's shoulder, trying to understand how the players would win or lose. In fact, she was attempting to understand what was happening on Billy's Apple iMac. So far, three medieval armoured soldiers stood guarding the gated entrance to the tower, to the left side of the screen. Above the guards, on the roof of the tower, tied securely to the flag pole, Martha was wriggling, in a vain attempt to free herself. But unseen by Martha and the three guards, a thick spiral of white smoke was slithering down from the top of the tower, moving towards the battlement floor.

Most of Billy's Apps allowed two players to compete. But it was clear from the complexity of *The Final Battle* that, with only minutes to cobble this App together, it would be one person, playing against the computer.

Now it was time to introduce the next and, hopefully, the saving grace: Axle and Imogena, also known as two fire-belching fully grown dragons. Their brief, programmed into the App, was to rescue the damsel in distress and to destroy, or permanently ensnare, the evil witch. Billy had allowed the witch to metamorphose into whatever forms she could achieve from her physical form, thus, adding more of a challenge for the scary dragons.

So, let battle commence! Billy could see that Gayla had already changed from her ugly human form into her successful slithering white smoke routine. But of course she would change. This was a fight to the end. There could only be one winner. Palogonia had to mirror the history books. Any other result would not only change Palogonian history, but the future of all those who followed.

1192 AD

Billy was right on the money. All they felt was a slight tingling as they were swept from Gerald's living room. Their electronic format landed them up against the right hand tower. Along the battlement walls, through the darkness, stood a corresponding tower. But they were no longer physical beings. On transfer from Gerald's room, Axle and Imogena were now electronic characters, completely under the control of a computer game player, somewhere in the future.

2016 AD

Billy was satisfied; all the players needed were locked into *The Final Battle*. All the combatants, awaiting instructions, were staring out from the screen of his Apple iMac. Apprehensively, Billy shuffled closer to the screen, poised and ready to commence battle. Being the only player, Billy chose the right hand side, fighting for the future of Palogonia; its future was now under his control. He knew full well that he would be challenged by Gayla's side, by attack programs which he'd already built in the App. If this had been real life, he'd certainly be on the side of the good guys. So Axle and Imogena, must be controlled by him, against the computer driving all the evils which Gayla could create.

Already, twenty extra soldiers had appeared on the left screen, each armed with flaming spears. Along the bottom of the screen, a numerically graded scale showed the extra lives gained from direct hits on the royal twins. For every direct hit, twenty extra-heavily-armed soldiers would appear, as an attack force for Gayla's battle.

But Billy had a response, eliminating the possibility of becoming overrun by killer soldiers. Axle was the first to be pushed into action. Using his second-level defence, Billy transformed his royal prince into a fully grown, flame-spitting dragon. As Billy's vengeful dragon moved across the battlements, flames began gushing across the screen. Instantly, all Gayla's soldiers were engulfed by the flames, disappearing from the screen. At the top of the screen, five golden crowns appeared, Axle's prize for defeating the soldiers.

But Billy had no time to enjoy his initial victory. From the side of the left-hand tower, a death-curdling scream could be heard. Billy watched, aware that Gayla had unused, life-threatening plans. As the shrieking continued, unfurling down the tower wall, a long white sheet appeared, displaying the new dangers about to be introduced. In blood red letters on a white sheet, the words explained all that was waiting to appear – *Tenatos joins the game – my pet Tyrannosaurus Rex – enjoy!*

1192 AD

Now free to explore, Jasper was attracted to a smaller doorway at the far extent of the room, where they'd been kept prisoner. Maybe it was a secret passageway, built to sneak surreptitiously between various rooms around the castle. Some hidden by doorways, carefully disguising tunnels, maintained as safe exit routes to the outside world, in the event of a surprise invasion. Once opened, their door exposed a small room with a large bed, fully covered with sheets and heavy woollen rugs. Along one wall, a number of shelves were laden with plates and pewter mugs. It was a secret hideaway, deep within the castle, with no external light or any form of heating: a perfect place to store the Queen, whilst they went searching for Gandolf's wife, Princess Xena.

Although men with a moral conscience, it was obviously going to be difficult to retain any sense of courtesy towards the wicked woman who was now cowering in the corner. A woman who carried total power outside this room, now begging for forgiveness. Until they'd found Princess Xena, there could be no discussion regarding her future; she was a woman renowned for her ruthless attitude towards all her citizens.

"You can make it easy for yourself. Just tell us where we find my wife." Gandolf moved close to his mother-in-law, struggling to retain an even temper, whilst thoughts of his wife's treatment by the woman facing him, began overpowering him.

"I will take you there. I can assure you my daughter is being well looked after. You know, she's been sick, so I had her placed in a special room, with the very best medical help," she lied, knowing that, once outside, she would scream for help. Within minutes, all three would be caught and unceremoniously tossed in the dungeons. Their deaths would be slow and painful.

"Your majesty, a wonderful story, but I'd never trusted you, even to cross the road. Your reputation goes before you. I think a short spell in the room which Jasper's found would be good. When we've found the Princess, well, maybe we'll think about what happens next." Gerald wanted to explain more of her misdemeanours and her brutality against her people, but there were more important fish to fry.

"She's too sick, she must be left alone, leave her. I beg you, as her mother. I'm pleading for her life, not mine," she began screaming, in a vain hope that she could convince them of her sincerity.

"The room it is." Gandolf took the lead, dragging the woman whom he hated more than he could express towards the door. With her inside the secret room, a thick wooden plank was wedged across, ensuring that the door was completely sealed tight.

With the Queen securely locked away, the first part of their search could start. But where? Where had Xena been imprisoned? For all the nonsense they'd heard, suggesting that she was under good medical care, was certainly complete and utter rubbish. Also, they had to search the East Wing of the castle, dodging the royal guards who could be aware that they had been held prisoner by the Queen. Maybe there was a possibility that the Queen had only used just a few of her close protection guards, leaving the men a better chance of moving undetected through the castle.

But irrespective of finding the imprisoned Princess, they were totally unaware of the conditions of the spell placed on Princess Xena by the old witch. Or indeed that she was cast within a spell. Or what was required to remove the spell. In fact, placing Gandolf's wedding band in his wife's left palm was the only action that would remove Gayla's spell. What was even more dangerous was that if the wedding band touched any other part of Princess Xena bare flesh, Gayla's spell would become permanent. Whilst they pondered their movements, Gayla was moving closer to her victory: a kingdom ruled over by 'Queen Gayla', a dynasty that would last for a thousand years.

2016 AD

From the smaller of his screens, Billy and Wendy watched on, as Gandolf forced Queen Ventenil, cursing and screaming, into the windowless room. Her voice disappeared, as the door slammed firmly shut.

"Wendy, whatd'you think? Should we interfere? Wendy?" Billy looked over his shoulder for answers to a conundrum facing his overall plan. But Wendy had decided that more wise words from Astrid were required. Astrid hovered at her usual level, just to Billy's left. Her pages were already open, glowing in the unlit room.

"Billy, a little more magic, if you please. We know that placing Gandolf's wedding band in Xena's left open palm will return Palogonia to its former glory, and documented history will return. Anything else, even placing it against her right palm, and the spell will stay forever. Then Gayla will become Queen and all our efforts will have been in vain. No, Billy, we've got to stop the boys before they cause irreparable damage. Can you move them to Gerald's room? Yes, of course you can. But one more thing, Billy; I don't know if you're this clever. Can you take the ring hanging on a string round Gandolf's neck? If you can, we can then save it for the children to carry out, killing the spell. Can you do it? Oh, and, make sure they're locked in Gerald's room until the App game's finished. I've got an idea how to deal with Gayla, permanently and humanely. Oh, and don't worry, once they're in Gerald's room, I'll remove Gerald's ability to move through time."

Gayla v Billy

From behind the tower, the screaming continued unabated. Eventually, Tenatos, Gayla's untested Tyrannosaurus alter ego, edged its way past the left-hand tower, into full view. Its mouth was wide open, exposing rows of triangular razor-sharp teeth. Waiting to select its next target, poised and ready for action, Tenatos stretched its body to expose its full height, reaching over half the height of Billy's screen.

"You're a big boy; now let's see what we can do with you, big feller," Billy placed his cursor on Princess Imogena, clicking twice. Instantly, a beautiful young girl was transformed into the second dragon, standing alongside her brother, already having successfully scored points, destroying all the heavily armed soldiers.

As Billy moved his two flaming dragons across the screen, Tenatos defiantly swung his head across to the top of the tower. Lowering his head against the flag pole, the snarling beast delicately grabbed Martha's clothing, lifting her from the flag pole. With its prey dangling from its bottom jaw, Tenatos took a few steps across the screen; Martha was suspended by her clothing beneath the monster's slobbering mouth.

Billy could sense his intricate programming working against him. As much as he wanted to engulf Tenatos with flames from two sides with his dragons, any attack would be the end of Martha. If Gayla, in the form of any of her alter egos, was victorious in the battle, he would have to allow the victor release from the App and back to their physical being. For Gayla, this would mean having ultimate control of Palogonia. Maybe Astrid might have the answer: cheating, maybe, but delivering the answer which Astrid had sought to this whole episode.

Billy scribbled away on his keyboard, writing a number of new lines of programming. There was a fifty-fifty chance, no more, that Astrid's idea would work. If it failed, Gayla would land smack back in the castle, no longer Queen Ventenil's servant, but ruler of the great kingdom of Palogonia.

In one click on the right hand button of his mouse, Billy's two dragons changed back into two royal princesses. But more tricks were ready. Martha had to be saved. Adding yet another special programme to the App, Gayla's hostage, suspended from the mouth of Tenatos, joined the royal twins, all three disappearing from *The Final Battle*. Tenatos screamed with fury, as Martha vanished from the screen. But with the deafening screams and wild movements, realising its prey had escaped, Tenatos's form began disolve into a hazy cloud of electronic dots. As the haze of dots cleared, there, leaning against the left hand tower, Gayla stood, starring out from the screen, pointing angrily towards Billy.

Billy's cursor hovered over Gayla, as she moved across the screen in a vain attempt to escape the inevitable. One click from his mouse was all that he needed.

1192 AD

Martha, Imogena and Axle, bumped along the floor into Gerald's quarters. Now back safely with their father, Jason and Gerald, together they could plan how to finish the horrors they had all be subjected to. But there were problems and dangers yet to overcome. As far as they knew, Gayla was still a danger. Plus, how could they trust Queen Ventenil?

"There's no need to fear, my friends," Astrid said, as she hovered from behind the curtains, moving closer to the six brave players, who had once been caught up in Gayla's evil attempt to take over Palogonia. "Billy has moved Gayla to another world."

"Gandolf, around your neck is your wedding band. All you have to do is place the band into your wife's left palm, nothing else Gandolf. Then all will be as it should be. Now go, and good luck my dear friends."

"Where's Billy? Is he OK?" Gerald moved towards his old friend. "I suppose my mind will be cleared, as will theirs?"

Astrid ruffled her pages, rubbing against her old friend. "Goodbye, Gerald."

CHAPTER FORTY-FOUR

Thanks Billy.
1192 AD
The Kingdom of Palogonia

Along with Billy, Gandolf, Wendy, her mother, Gerald, and Jasper, looked on in disbelief at the burnt remains, that once had been the generational home of the Castleman family. So intense had been the flames that snow piled high nearby had melted, flooding two nearby vegetable gardens and a neighbour's low-lying house. Since Gandolf had rescued his wife, just as Astrid had predicted, life had returned as set out in Billy's research from Wikipedia. It was as though the lights had been turned back on, with life for all rekindled to its previous quality, with smiling faces openly visible across the kingdom. Those with Billy today understood that the years controlled by Gayla's spells were just a bad dream. But Billy was fully aware that his friends must also have their memories expunged. Time travel, and witches' spells, must never again exist in Palogonia. Now that the mirage spell cast over the kingdom, created by Gayla, had been lifted, several other witches had also been expelled from Palogonia. Gayla, the evilness behind the black cloud that hung over Palogonia, was now a series of electronic bytes, unceremoniously dumped somewhere within a deleted computer game. A million light years from Palogonia, and the prosperous and happy life that now existed in 1192 AD.

As the friends walked along the busy village street, once again children's laughter and the calls from hordes of thriving market traders filled the air. Gandolf had never experienced the sounds of the village folk. He had never been allowed to journey amongst the villagers, loyal citizens who had made Palogonia the power which it had become under King Bresdon. Ahead of their group, voices from the crowds along the main street increased. Outside the local tavern, colourfully-adorned Morris dancers spun around a decorated Maypole. Their audience captured the mood, singing along with the syncopated rhythm created by dozens of sticks, tapped furiously against the stone walls.

Billy had never reached the outskirts of the village bordered by the fast flowing River Palo. A simple wooden bridge, crossing the river, marked the limit of the village, and the only entry point into the village from the southern extreme of the castle. Looking back across the landscape towards the castle, imperiously standing high above the village, Billy marvelled at the beauty of the imposing kingdom that had become an intrinsic part of his last few weeks.

In the distance, approaching the river bridge, a line of mounted soldiers were slowly approaching at walking pace. Each soldier was proudly wearing the red cross on a badly soiled white tunic. Ahead of the group, a crusader's flag, matching their soiled tunics, was proudly being held aloft by one of the leading troopers.

Two by two, the crusaders crossed the narrow bridge; dozens of muddied hooves clattered against the timber structure. Billy moved to allow the procession of crusaders uninterrupted passage, standing in awe of the powerful unit of exhausted soldiers.

As the troopers approached Billy and his friends, the flag-bearer raised his hand bringing the troop to a halt. Across the crowded roadway, those fit and able dropped on one knee, their heads respectively bent towards the troop of crusaders.

"So you are the famous Billy, who has helped save my friend's nation." One of the riders edged towards Billy, sliding from his restless white stallion. Billy was now the only able-bodied man still standing upright.

"I'm sorry, but..." Billy stuttered, confused at events unfolding around him.

Another crusader eased himself from his jet black stallion, joining Billy and the other crusader.

"Young man please let me introduce King Richard. I think you'll know him as Richard the Lionheart. Oh, and I'm King Bresdon." The King of Palogonia eased Billy closer to King Richard.

"Excuse me, sir, I mean your majesties," Billy struggled to know what to say. Was this his dream sequence? "It'll take too long to explain my being here your majesty, I've just helped out, and nothing will have changed."

King Richard eased Billy by the arm, leading him away from his fellow soldiers, leaving Billy's friends staring at the rapidly unfolding events, with a degree of shock. As King Richard and Billy walked away from the bridge into an adjoining meadow, no one moved to follow them. Across the countryside, most of the previous day's blizzard had melted. As though they were two old friends, strolling for a morning expedition to review the readiness of the land, Billy and the Lionheart ambled along the river bank. Billy understood that this must be his brush with destiny.

"It's OK, Billy Chen, Astrid and I have met before. I understand that all the memories of my people will be taken. You will have never existed. But we both know that the history of this great kingdom has been protected. Maybe we shall meet again, young Billy Chen. Now can I suggest you rub your thumbnails together and request a homeward trip. Goodbye, my friend; and thank you again."

Leaving Billy unsure what to say, King Richard turned, pacing back along the river's edge towards his troop. As though he'd forgotten something, he turned towards Billy. "And send my thanks to Astrid, if you would be so kind, Billy Chen."

BILLY'S NEXT ADVENTURE
Billy Chen and the Astral Plane

During World War II, Colonel Herman Guntfeld has discovered the ability to move freely across time, using the mystical Astral Plane. Relying on his top secret methods, Colonel Guntfeld now has the ability to look down unhindered on Winston Churchill's war plans. Hitler's number one spy obtains access to secret documents which Mr Churchill and his allied friends are preparing for the D-Day landings.

Astrid asks Billy to intervene, and stop the German from ruining the allied plans to save Europe. From the initial information which Billy collects, it appears that Germany has the war already won, defying documented history.

But Billy and Astrid have a plan to remove Colonel Guntfeld's access to his secret Astral Plane travel loop. Twenty-first century technology again steps in on Billy's side.